VANISHING HOUSE

J.Taghavi

Tellwell Talent
www.tellwell.ca

ISBN
978-1-77370-421-0 (Paperback)

Table of Contents

PART 1

Desert

1

JEAN, A FORTY-THREE YEAR OLD HOUSEWIFE, LIVED IN A town near New York City along with her two children: Lucy, who was eight years old, and George, who was 15. There wasn't, however, a man of the house anymore – Jean and her husband had separated due to irreconcilable differences, and soon afterwards he'd moved in with his mother, leaving Jean alone with the kids. It was a tough life, but she was slowly getting used to it.

One frosty winter's morning, Jean's alarm clock went off – as usual – at 7 a.m., suddenly rousing her from a deep sleep. She got out of bed as quickly as she could, shivering in the cold as she rushed out of her room and into her daughter's bedroom next door.

"Get up!" Jean yelled at Lucy, waking her up. "It's time to go to school!"

Covering her head with the blanket, Lucy mumbled, "I don't want to go; please let me have a day off!"

Jean groaned; her daughter was always trying to get out of going to school. "Lucy, get up right now!" she ordered in her harshest voice as she yanked back the blanket. "You're going to school and that's final!"

Muttering under her breath, Jean made her way over to her son's room to wake him too, and when George replied – in a rather sleepy voice – that he was going to get up, she left him to his own devices and headed downstairs. She could hear George heading into the bathroom, and satisfied that her children were doing as they were supposed to be doing, she started cooking breakfast.

Not long afterwards George came down, saying "Good morning" to his mother – who smiled in response – and sitting down at the large kitchen table.

At least her son was on time, she thought, and upon realising that her daughter still hadn't left her bedroom, Jean shouted up the stairs, "Lucy, hurry up and get down here!" It was always the same, every single morning, and it was getting tiring.

Eventually Lucy emerged from her room, whining and moaning about how early it was as she made her way down the stairs and sat next to her brother. He just rolled his eyes in response. Moments later Jean finished preparing the cooked breakfast – eggs, sausages, tomatoes, and beans – placing it in front of George before putting some cereal and milk onto the table for Lucy.

Picking up the milk, Lucy stared at her mother, her eyebrows raised. "You know I don't like milk; why do I have to have cereal?" she whined.

Jean sighed as she explained, "Because, as I keep telling you, milk is good for you; it gives you energy and helps you concentrate. So eat up!"

Clearly not convinced, Lucy completely ignored the cereal and instead placed some sausages and eggs in front of her, stealing them from her brother's plate. Jean frowned as she watched this happen – couldn't her daughter listen to her, just for once? It was so exhausting to keep battling with her like this!

Trying hard to keep her calm, Jean sat down next to her children, watching them eat with a mixture of love and exasperation. Suddenly, she remembered that her mother was coming over later – as if she could forget. "Your grandmother is coming to see us today," she told Lucy and George, "so please come straight home after school – don't be late, will you?"

That, at least, put a smile on Lucy's face. "Oh, I've missed Grandma so much!" she exclaimed. "I can't wait to see her!"

After breakfast, a much happier Lucy put on her school uniform, said goodbye to her mum, and left the house, immediately seeing one of her friends on the other side of the road. "Liza, Liza!" she called excitedly. "My grandmother is seeing me today!" She smiled widely as they carried on walking to school. "I can't wait to see what present she brings me this time!"

Meanwhile, back at home, George also said goodbye to his mother, and after taking his bike from the garage, he rode off to his own school, thinking about the day ahead.

Jean watched him go, smiling at how big her son was growing, before getting started on the housework: dusting every room, mopping all the floors, and washing the dishes – she wanted everything to be absolutely spick and span for when her mother came.

* * *

A few hours later the doorbell rang, making Jean smile widely as she rushed over to open the door. As ever, she was just as excited to spend time with her mother as her kids were, and when she saw her standing there on the doorstep, she leaned in for a hug before kissing her on the cheek.

"Welcome, come in, come in!" she exclaimed, and her mother – Mary – followed her inside.

"How are you, dear?" she asked Jean, "And how are the children? They're at school now, I suppose?"

Jean nodded. "They are indeed, and I told them to come home straight away – they're both eager to see you again. Come on," she added, "sit down at the table and I'll make you a nice cup of tea."

As Jean put the kettle on and got the teacups ready, Mary started asking questions. "So, what's happening with your husband? Does he come to see the children often?" She said the words quite casually, but Jean knew that her mother was dying to know what was going on.

She shook her head. "No, he doesn't. In fact, he hasn't come round since our last argument, which was about three weeks ago now." She sighed. "He does call occasionally though, to speak to the kids."

Mary sighed too. "It's not right! Children should be able to see their own father; they need that male role model in their lives. I hope that one day the two of you can come to your senses and solve your problems, I really do."

Jean busied herself with making the tea, not wanting to look her mother in the eye as she replied, "Well, there's not much I can do about that, but the kids will see their father soon – Shawn's taking them to the funfair to spend some time with them. George wanted to go and shoot the clay pigeons there."

"Oh, that's wonderful!" exclaimed Mary, suddenly becoming very animated indeed. "And who knows, maybe you'll start to get closer with Shawn again too, the more time he spends with the kids."

Tears formed in Jean's eyes then; she knew how much her mother wanted her to make up with Shawn, but it just wasn't that simple. And it wasn't up to her anyway! "Well, I highly doubt that, considering he's seeing another woman." She paused, trying to pull herself together. "I just can't bear to see him – I keep picturing him with *her*. I don't understand… how, after sixteen years, can he be unfaithful to me?" She turned and looked at Mary, pleading her mum to give her some kind of answer.

"Oh, darling, don't get upset," she replied. "I know it's hard, but I really believe he regrets what happened – he even called me to explain how sorry he was for what he did. Now, you can't change the past, but you *can* decide on how you move forward in the future. You just need to calm down and sort it out; there's no need to carry on like this."

Jean sighed as she took the teacups over to the table. "Maybe you're right, mother, maybe you're right."

Mary smiled. "Aren't I always?"

* * *

A few hours later the doorbell rang, and telling Jean to sit and relax, Mary went to open it. She knew it would be Lucy, and when she saw her granddaughter standing outside, she pulled her in for kisses and cuddles. "Oh, I missed you, Lucy! I'm so glad to see you, darling!"

Lucy was clearly delighted to see her grandmother, and as they made their way into the living room to join Jean, she said, "Me too, Grandma! I've missed you so much." She grinned up at Mary. "By the way, I was wondering if you'd brought me a present."

Jean laughed, though she was shaking her head in exasperation. "Lucy! You shouldn't say things like that." She turned to face her mother. "I'm sorry; children are always after materialistic items rather than kindness."

"No, not particularly," Mary replied. "Most children are after both."

Jean laughed again. "Yeah, I guess that's true!"

Lucy had been looking back and forth between her mother and her grandmother, and upon hearing this she exclaimed, "No Mum, that's not right! I love my grandma with my whole heart!"

Mary pressed her hand to her chest, clearly touched, but Jean wasn't having any of it. "Well then, Lucy, why is it – if you care about her so much – that the first thing you asked your grandma about was your present?"

Lucy, who looked genuinely ashamed, turned to Mary with her head hung low as she whispered, "I'm sorry, Grandma; I shouldn't have asked you that."

"Don't worry Lucy," she replied, patting her gently on the shoulder. "As it happens, I do have a present for you. Here." Mary took a book from her bag, along with a pair of earrings in a jewellery box, and handed them over to her granddaughter, whose shameful look had now vanished completely and had been replaced by a huge, wide smile. "I got you a book about reptiles because I know how much you're interested in them," Mary explained.

Without waiting another moment, Lucy grabbed the book and started eagerly flicking through its pages, her eyes growing large in wonder as she saw all the many photographs and illustrations. "Look at this snake, Mum! It's so beautiful!" She thrust the book under her mother's nose, making her cringe back into her seat.

"Oh Lucy, take that away from me – you know how frightened I am of snakes!"

Mary laughed, taking a seat next to her daughter. "Same for me I'm afraid, Lucy – I'm scared of snakes as well. In fact, I didn't even bother looking through the book. I hope it's a good one."

Lucy grinned, amused at the idea that anyone could be scared of snakes, and then decided to change the subject. "How's your cat, Grandma?" Lucy always asked about her cat whenever she saw her.

Mary sighed. "I tell you, it feels like that cat is getting older than me! I don't know what he does all day – he leaves the house in the morning and doesn't come back until the night time." She smiled. "Of course, since he's finding his own food I don't have to spend much money on him!"

Lucy laughed before excusing herself. "If it's OK with you, Grandma, I want to go to my room and start reading my book now."

Mary patted her on the shoulder again. "Of course, darling. Enjoy your snakes!"

After heading upstairs and flicking through the book for a few minutes, Lucy started thinking about her brother. Where was he? Their mum had told them to get straight back home after school to see Grandma, but he was nowhere to be found. He must be hanging out with his friends, thought

Lucy, a deliciously naughty thought forming in her mind. If he couldn't be bothered to come and see Grandma, maybe Lucy would have to go and remind him!

Taking her earrings out of the jewellery box Grandma had given her, Lucy went over to her chest of baby things – objects her mother hadn't thrown away from when Lucy was younger – and pulled out one of her old dummies. Then, placing it in the box, she found some fancy paper to wrap it in, finishing the whole thing by putting a decorative bow on the top. It looked perfect.

Heading downstairs, she paused to see where her mum and grandma were, and after realising they were out in the back garden, she walked over to the front door and let herself out. Sure enough, she could see her brother hanging out with his girlfriend and two of his mates at the end of the road, where there was a little park situated next to the pavement.

Walking over to them, Lucy held out the little box. "George," she said, "I thought you were coming back to see Grandma?" She shrugged. "Well, since you weren't at home, she gave your present to me to give to you. Here it is, be careful not to lose it. I hope you like it – I got some *very* nice earrings." She managed to hand over the 'gift' without laughing, but as soon as she turned and walked away from her brother, she couldn't help the little giggle that escaped through her lips. "I'll see you at home!" she called over her shoulder, before walking back to the house.

George turned back to his friends, frowning as he said, "I completely forgot Grandma was coming to see us – I'd better get back home."

"Let's see what you got first," his girlfriend said, gesturing at the box. "It looks like it could be expensive."

"Yeah, it could be a gold watch or something," one of his mates said. "Go on, open it up!"

Now with an excited smile on his face, George unwrapped the present, grinning at his friends as the little red jewellery box was revealed. It must be a watch, he thought to himself happily, but when he pried open the lid of the box and saw what was inside, his cheeks went bright red.

George's friends and his girlfriend – all of whom had been watching his every move – burst out laughing upon seeing the dummy, and one of his mates even started making gurgling baby noises.

Mortified, George got on his bike without a word, riding off towards his house without even saying goodbye to his friends. He could still hear them laughing in the distance when he got to his door, and as he let himself into the house, he muttered under his breath, "Lucy, I'm going to *kill* you!"

His sister was standing in the hallway, looking at George as though she didn't know what was wrong, but when he darted towards her, she turned and ran up the stairs, rushing into her bedroom and locking the door quickly behind her.

Still in the garden, his mother and grandmother didn't see any of this, and George took the opportunity to run after his sister without them trying to stop him. When he got to her door he began banging and kicking on the wooden surface, daring Lucy to open it and let him in, and getting angrier and angrier when she wouldn't.

"What on earth is going on?" Jean yelled from the hallway, having finally realised there was something happening inside the house. "What happened?" she asked as she walked upstairs, heading over to George and grabbing him by the arm. "What are you doing?"

Tears sprung to George's eyes then – tears of humiliation rather than anything else – and he went and sat on the top step of the stairs, burying his head in his hands. "Lucy embarrassed me in front of everyone – I won't be able to face them after this. How can I even show my face at school?"

Jean frowned. "What did she do? Tell me, George," she said softly, sitting down next to her son and trying to comfort him.

Rather reluctantly he started telling his mum the story, but when he got to the bit about opening the present in front of his mates and his girlfriend, his voice failed him.

"What was it?" she asked, absolutely baffled as to where this was going.

He shook his head, too embarrassed to say what was in the box, but Jean reached out and squeezed his hand. "I won't be able to punish Lucy if you don't tell me," she explained, something that seemed to get through to him.

"OK," he replied, inhaling deeply and letting out a large breath before admitting, "It was a dummy."

Jean looked down at her lap, as though she were angry, when in reality she was just trying to stop herself from laughing out loud – the last thing she wanted to do was humiliate her son further, even if the whole thing *was* pretty funny. "Don't worry," she said, once she'd got herself under control, "I'll punish Lucy. And I'm sure your friends will be fine; there's no need to avoid them."

Just then Grandma appeared at the bottom of the stairs, peering up at the two of them as she called, "Hello! What are you doing up there?"

Leaning over to George, Jean whispered, "Why don't you go and talk to your grandma? I'll go and speak with Lucy."

Nodding, George wiped the remaining tears from his face before heading downstairs to greet his grandmother. They exchanged hugs and kisses, and then Mary held him at arm's length so she could get a good look at him. "You know George, every time I see you, you just get bigger and bigger! Tell me, did you have a good day at school?"

George's smile immediately dropped from his face, and when he lowered his head in sadness, Mary asked, "What happened, George? Are you OK?"

"Yes, Grandma," he replied automatically, and then, wanting to change the subject, he quickly brought up the fact he was hanging out with his dad at the fair the next day. "We're going shooting," he said excitedly.

Mary nodded. "Your father is a good shot; I happen to know he's won many prizes over the years. You can learn a lot from him."

George smiled. "I hope so!"

2

THE NEXT DAY — WHICH WAS A SATURDAY — THE CHIL-
dren got up early, making sure they were washed, dressed,
and ready to go before the doorbell rang.

Lucy, who had soon got over the telling off she'd had
from her mum regarding the dummy, rushed over to the
door excitedly, jumping for joy when she saw her father on
the doorstep. "Daddy!" she exclaimed happily as she hugged
him tightly.

Just then Mary appeared in the hallway, looking out at
Shawn, who was smiling at his daughter. "What are you
doing out there? Come inside for a minute. Jean's in the
kitchen; we're just having a cup of tea."

Shawn shook his head. "Thanks but we'd better make a
move before the traffic gets too heavy."

"Don't you want to talk to Mum?" Lucy asked her
father, frowning.

"Of course I do," Shawn replied, ruffling Lucy's head with his right hand, "just not right now – don't you want to get to the fair before it gets really busy?"

Lucy thought about this for a moment, then nodded. "Maybe you can see her later instead?" she suggested.

Ignoring his daughter's question, Shawn held out a key ring and said, "Now, can you do me a little favour? Can you take these keys to George and tell him to get the shotguns from the gun case? We need number 1 and 4."

Happy to have been given a job to do, Lucy took the keys and ran upstairs, giving them to George and passing on the message. George nodded briefly, taking the keys from her without saying a word – he still hadn't quite forgiven her for her little dummy prank the day before.

He went over to the gun case in the spare room, unlocked it, and took out the guns, holding them carefully as he walked downstairs and handed them to his father. "Hey Dad, here you go. Did you want me to get the bullets as well?"

Shawn shook his head. "No need, son – the place we're going provides them so we don't need to take our own. Now, are you both ready for a day of adventure?"

Lucy jumped up and down while George nodded and smiled, and after saying a quick goodbye to Mary – who was still hovering in the hallway – he led his kids over to his car, which was parked at the side of the road. "Let Lucy sit in the front," he told George as he opened the door, "I don't have the patience to hear you both bickering about where you want to sit, OK?"

"OK Dad," George replied as Lucy got into the passenger seat with a big, smug smile on her face – it was as if she'd 'won' a game George hadn't been aware of playing, and he shook his head as he sat in the back.

Shawn waved goodbye to Mary – who by now was standing in the doorway – before driving off, while from the kitchen window, Jean watched them go. She wished she could have gone with them.

Back in the car, after Shawn had asked the kids how things were going at school and if they were keeping up with their homework, Lucy suddenly blurted out, "When are you going to come back home, Dad? Do you still not like Mum?"

From the backseat, George muttered, "Don't ask questions like that, Lucy."

Lucy was just about to turn around and ask her brother why not when their dad replied, "It's OK, George. Don't worry about us, Luce, we'll sort things out eventually. Sometimes people just need a bit of time apart. It'll all be fine, I promise. And I *do* like your Mum, so don't be thinking otherwise."

Lucy nodded, though she wasn't sure whether she believed him or not, and the three of them spent the rest of the drive in silence. They drove out of the town and into the countryside, and soon they found themselves at the funfair, which was already pretty busy with lots of adults and children milling around the games machines, booths, and food stalls.

The various smells of the delicious fair food hit them as soon as they got out of the car, and Lucy's mouth immediately started watering as Shawn took the guns out and locked the doors. "Right, me and George are going to do some shooting practice," he said to his daughter. "If you don't wish to come with us, you can wander about and see what you'd like to do. But be careful – don't wander too far. Stay to the main fair area, OK?"

Lucy frowned as she looked at the guns he was carrying. "No Dad, I want to learn how to shoot too!"

George rolled his eyes. "You're too small to handle the guns, Lucy – you won't be able to manage them."

Sensing the start of an argument, Shawn interrupted before it could escalate any further. "OK, Lucy, why don't you come with us and you can watch us practice? Then we'll see how it goes."

Smiling excitedly, Lucy followed her father and brother over to the shooting range, and even though she was indeed too young to be able to fire the gun, Shawn taught her how to hold it properly, which made her feel a little bit grown up at least.

George, however, had been practising for years, and needed no help from his dad as he held up the gun and shot at the target. He was pretty good at it too, if he did say so himself.

Lucy watched her brother shoot for a few minutes, but she soon got bored, and turning to her dad she asked, "Isn't there anything else I can use? A smaller shotgun or something? *Please?*"

"I'm afraid not," Shawn said, patting her on the head. "You're still a bit too young, Luce – you'll need to wait a few more years until you can start learning properly." He thought of what Jean would say if he let Lucy fire a gun, trying not to smile as he imagined her reaction; she would go through the roof!

By now Lucy was in full-on moping mode, and getting more and more angry by the whole situation, she decided she didn't want to stay there for even a second longer. "I'm bored," she told her dad, "I'm going to go and get some ice cream."

"OK Luce, but be careful," Shawn replied, watching her go. He never worried about her going off on her own – she was always cautious around strangers, he knew. Or at least, he thought he knew.

Lucy wandered around the stalls for a while – trying not to think of how George got to do everything she didn't – and as she walked towards one of the outdoor games, she happened to notice a rather striking man heading towards her. He was very short with a long, white beard and wonderful colourful robes that hung right down to the ground.

Walking over to the man, she looked up and asked, "Are you a fortune teller?" Lucy would very much have liked to have her fortune told, especially if it involved her somehow getting one over on her brother.

The man – who up close, looked quite old – shook his head as he reached for his walking stick. "No, my girl," he replied, his voice low and rather mysterious, "I am not a fortune teller. I do, however, know things about the past and the future."

Lucy considered this for a moment before taking a step closer and asking, "If I give you some pieces of chocolate, can you predict my future for me?"

The old man laughed, shaking his head again. "Thank you for your kindness, my dear, but I'm afraid I do not like chocolate."

Lucy's eyes widened – she'd never met anyone who didn't like chocolate. "OK… well… how about if I gave you a biscuit instead?" There couldn't be anyone who didn't like either chocolate or biscuits, could there?

The old man smiled. "My girl, you seem to have a good heart and are very kind. Thank you for your offer, but I'm afraid I'm simply not a fortune teller. Now if you'll excuse me, I must be on my way…"

A rather disappointed Lucy watched as the man hobbled away, leaning on his walking stick, but soon her spirits were raised by the sight of the ice cream van. After purchasing her favourite ice cream, she started making her way back to the shooting range, but when she was only halfway there she encountered three boys about her own age, who were hassling the old man she'd met just moments before.

"Why are you bothering him?" she shouted as she ran over, throwing the rest of her ice cream at one of the boys before adding, "Leave him alone! Don't you have anything better to do?"

The boy – who had been hit right in the face by the fast flying ice cream – started towards Lucy, but stopped when the sound of a man's voice floated over to them. "Come on boys, let's go home!"

He turned to see his father, along with the parents of his friends, and sighed in frustration; they couldn't exactly retaliate when they were being watched. As they walked away, however, one of the boys turned to Lucy and said, "Watch out for your grandfather, won't ya? He wouldn't be able to get out of a pit if he fell in one!"

Lucy watched them go – proud of herself for standing up to them – and once they'd left, the old man turned to her, a grateful expression on his face. "Thank you for saving me from those little devils," he said as he sat down on a nearby rock. Lucy went and sat beside him. "Now, I have a secret to tell you that may well make you very happy. Do you want to hear it?"

Lucy nodded eagerly. "Yes, please tell me!" she exclaimed happily, wondering if she was about to have her future told after all.

Smiling, the old man took a small, ancient-looking stone tablet out of his robes. It had tiny words engraved into it that Lucy couldn't see from where she sat. "First," he said, "put this stone tablet in a bucket of water, and then with that water, mark out the boundaries of your house. Then you'll need to put the stone somewhere safe – hide it away so no one can find it."

Lucy nodded, even though she had no idea why the man was telling her any of this.

"This stone will help you travel wherever you want to go, as well as the rest of your family; whenever you see lightning, put this tablet in a bucket of water and say "Ahora" three times before proclaiming your wish of where you want to go – any-where in the world." The old man smiled before adding, "Not only can this tablet take you to different *parts* of the world, it can also take you to different *times*."

Lucy looked at the tablet, frowning, then back up at the man. He seemed sincere enough, but what he was saying couldn't possibly be true, could it? This piece of stone couldn't possibly be magical… could it?

Before she knew it the man was saying goodbye, and after watching him hobble off, she looked down at the tablet again. She didn't for a second believe it could transport her and her family anywhere, but she supposed it could be worth a few dollars, so she put it in her pocket before heading back to the shooting range.

Before she could even get there, however, George appeared in front of her, and he looked angry. "Where have you been? You're late!" he hissed.

Lucy grinned. "Oh, thanks for your concern for your little sister!"

George laughed. "I'm only here because Dad sent me to look for you – personally, I couldn't care less what happened to you." He was still thinking of the dummy prank, and Lucy knew it.

She was about to reply when she saw something over George's shoulder – a girl and a boy a few yards away, who seemed to be hiding behind a tree. The girl looked remarkably like George's girlfriend. "Isn't that Nicole?" she asked, pointing at the tree.

George instinctively turned around to look, then shrugged before turning back to Lucy. "Of course it's not Nicole! Stop trying to play stupid pranks on me; it's not funny!"

Lucy sighed – George was either short-sighted or in denial – and then, to prove her point, she shouted out, "Nicole!"

At the sound of her name the girl stepped out fully from behind the tree, looking around to see who was calling her, and when her gaze fell on Lucy and George, she froze.

George, upon seeing that it was indeed his girlfriend, started to blush a furious shade of red. Then, turning his back on Nicole, he whispered to his sister in a rather shaky voice, "Come on, Dad's waiting for us."

Seeing how upset her brother was, Lucy tried to back-track. "It might not be Nicole; it could be someone else. Maybe I made a mistake," she suggested, though she knew it was pointless.

They started walking off together in silence, George either too angry or devastated to say anything, and soon they were getting into the car with their dad, who immediately started driving them back home.

"So, did you have a good day?" Shawn asked his children, smiling at Lucy and then catching George's eye in the rear view mirror.

Shifting in her seat, Lucy answered for the both of them. "Well, *I* had a good time, but I'm not sure if George did."

Shawn laughed. "What? Of course he had a good day, didn't you, George? We had fun shooting." He grinned at his son in the mirror. "You're a very good shooter, a natural. Did you know that?"

There was a pause before George replied, his voice still shaky as he replied, "Yes, father." He was clearly still thinking about his girlfriend, and realising that his son was upset about something, Shawn left him alone.

The three of them passed the rest of the journey in silence, and when they'd got home and had got out of the car, Shawn kissed Lucy before saying goodbye. Once she'd run into the house, he turned to George. "Take the shotguns and put them back in the case – and don't forget to lock it when you're done."

George nodded, still saying nothing, and Shawn reached out to pat him on the back. "Whatever it is, it'll be alright," he told his son, before getting in his car and driving off.

Jean stood up from the kitchen table when she heard her kids getting home, giving them each a hug as she asked, "So, did you have a good day with your Dad?"

"Oh yes, Mum, we had a great time!" Lucy exclaimed, and Jean was so focused on her daughter that she didn't notice the tiny, miniscule shrug that George gave in response.

"Now, go and get changed before dinner – Grandma's cooking tonight!" Jean said, looking extremely excited; it wasn't often she got a night off from making the dinner.

Lucy bounded upstairs, still full of energy even after the long car journey, and as she started getting undressed in her bedroom, the stone tablet fell out of her pocket, landing with a clunk on the floor. She stared at it for a moment, remembering what the old man had told her, and after deliberating for a minute or two, she decided to give it a go – what was the worst that could happen?

After finding a bucket in the spare room, she filled it with water from the bathroom and then placed the stone inside, watching it fall to the bottom. Creeping out of her bedroom, she then made sure the coast was clear before running down the stairs and out the front door, where she proceeded to mark out the perimeter of the house. Satisfied that she'd done a good job, she went and took a quick shower before dinner.

Jean was helping Mary set the table when Lucy appeared, and after serving out the food, they all sat down. George was already there, staring miserably down at his lap.

"I hope you enjoy!" said Mary, as she opened up her napkin and placed it on her legs.

"I'm sure I will," replied Lucy enthusiastically. "You know I love your cooking!"

Mary laughed before glancing at George, who was saying nothing. She could tell something was wrong with him but she didn't want to pry – sometimes teenage boys just needed their space.

Jean also noticed that her son was particularly quiet all throughout dinner, and when he'd finished eating, he simply said, "I'm tired," before heading off to his room. Jean and Mary exchanged a worried look.

When Lucy had finished her meal she thanked her grandma and then settled down to watch television. It wasn't long, however, before she started yawning, so saying goodnight, she too headed off to bed.

Lucy fell asleep straight away, but it was a rather restless sleep, and eventually – at around 2 a.m. – she woke up, the sound of thunder filling her little room. She could see bright flashes of lightning pouring in through the gap in her curtains, and suddenly she remembered what the old man had told her: that if there was lightning, she could go wherever she wanted to in the world – she just needed to say "Ahora" three times.

At the fair she'd found the man's words hard to believe, but right now, in the middle of the night, with the lightning flashing into her room, it seemed all too easy to imagine he'd been speaking the truth.

Excited, Lucy leapt out of bed, rushing over to the window to watch the bolts of lightning for a moment, smiling as she did so. Yes, this would be the perfect time to test the tablet and see if the man had been telling the truth.

So, taking the tablet from under the bed where she'd been hiding it, she plopped it into the bucket of water she'd left in her room from earlier – as if she somehow knew there would be lightning tonight – and then, leaning over it, she whispered the word "Ahora" three times, her heart hammering in her chest as she waited to see what would happen.

After thinking about where she'd like to go, she closed her eyes and imagined a hot, sunny place, with hills of sand she could roll down and play with. She wished with all her heart that she could be there right now, and then she opened her eyes again.

Nothing happened.

She didn't know what she'd been expecting, exactly — whether a loud bang or a flash of light or the room suddenly swirling around her — but there was nothing.

Annoyed (both that the tablet hadn't worked and that she'd been silly enough to believe the old man in the first place), Lucy got back into bed. "What a waste of time!" she muttered to herself, closing her eyes and going straight back to sleep — all that excitement and anticipation had made her exhausted.

Once Lucy was asleep again the tablet inside the bucket started glowing, a bright beam of light shooting out of the container and dashing out the window. If Lucy had been watching, she'd have seen the light from the tablet reach the lightning in the distance, the two beams crashing into each other and exploding in the night.

If she hadn't been sound asleep at that moment, Lucy would also have seen the light from the explosion refract onto the water she'd used to mark the perimeter of the house, making the liquid glow from within. This glow got brighter and brighter, and stronger and stronger, and soon the light was so strong it began to actually pick up the entire house.

Throughout it all, Lucy slept on…

3

THE NEXT MORNING, THERE WAS SO MUCH LIGHT STREAM-ing in through the windows that Lucy was woken up far earlier than usual. She thought it was a little strange, but when she remembered getting up in the middle of the night and looking out at the lightning, she realised she must have left the curtains wide open. It was rather hot in her room, too, but she didn't think too much about it – perhaps her mum had got cold and turned the heating up.

Laughing at herself for her silliness – thinking that bit of stone was somehow going to transport her somewhere exotic! – she got out of bed, rubbing the sleep from her eyes as she stood up.

She caught a glimpse of something out of the corner of her eye, something that made her rush over to the window as fast as she could, and when she looked out, she couldn't believe her what she was seeing.

Instead of the usual view of her street and the houses opposite, Lucy could see sand – sand as far as the eye could see. It was a desert. "Sand!" she shouted, her heart thumping madly again. "It's sand! The old man was right! He must be a wizard!"

Lucy took one last look out the window before running out of her room, pausing on the landing to listen for a moment – there were no sounds at all; she was the only one up.

Running down the stairs, so fast she almost tripped, Lucy then walked down the hallway towards the front door, where she could see the bright light of the desert seeping in through the gaps of the door, not to mention the windows. It just seemed so warm and inviting, and when she reached out and opened the front door, the light filtered in, engulfing the entire house.

She ran outside without even stopping to put on some shoes, revelling in the way the warm sand felt beneath her feet as she ran up a nearby sand dune. When she reached the top of the hill, Lucy took a moment to look out at her surroundings, pinching herself to make sure she wasn't dreaming. It was definitely real. The house was in the middle of nowhere, with nothing and no one else around it but desert – it was so beautiful. Screaming with delight, she then lay on the sand and rolled down the hill. It was as fun as she'd expected it to be, and she couldn't wait to show her family.

Running back inside, she yelled up the stairs, "Get up! Everyone, get out of bed right now! You have to see this!" She paused, waiting for a response, and when none came she added, "We're in the middle of a desert!"

Getting frustrated that no one was replying, Lucy ran up the stairs and headed straight for her mother's bedroom, banging the door open in her excitement. "Mum!" she yelled. "Look where we are! Sand, sand, and more sand… the house is surrounded by sand!"

Still sleepy, Jean slowly opened her eyes and focused on her daughter. "What are you shouting about? Why are you up so early?" She looked Lucy up and down. "And why are your pyjamas so dirty?"

Lucy sighed. "I've been trying to tell you – it's sand! I rolled down a huge hill of it! Just get up and have a look!"

Jean frowned as she dragged herself out of bed. "What's got into you? Why would you be playing in sand this early in the morning?" She paused then, her gaze moving to the radiator. "It sure is hot today; I'd better go and turn off the heating."

Lucy stamped her foot on the floor, frustrated that no one was listening to her. "The heating has nothing to do with it," she tried to explain, "it's just the weather!"

"What on earth are you talking about?"

Just then, Mary appeared in the doorway behind Lucy, having heard all the commotion. "Why is it so hot in here?" she asked, fanning herself with her hand. "Why is the heating up so high?"

Lucy turned to her grandma, hoping she'd listen to her. "We're in the desert!" she explained. "Just look out the window and you'll see what I mean!"

"Oh dear," said Mary, exchanging a worrying look with Jean. "Are you alright, Lucy? I hope you're not sick…" Her eyes widened then. "I hope it wasn't my dinner that made you sick!"

Lucy stamped her foot on the floor again, now utterly and completely exasperated that no one was listening to her. Then, realising that actions might speak louder than words, she ran downstairs, flung all the curtains open in all the rooms, and opened the front door wide.

From the doorway of Jean's room, Mary and her daughter could see the bright light coming from downstairs, and after exchanging another look – this time of confusion – they both headed down to the hallway.

Lucy was waiting for them next to the front door. "Go on, go outside and see where we are."

At first Jean flinched away from the light, but upon seeing the look on Lucy's face, she walked towards the door and headed outside to investigate.

She stared at the mounds of sand surrounding the house, holding her hands up to her forehead to protect her eyes from the glare as she asked, "What on earth…?" Mary came out of the house then, and Jean turned to face her mother. "Am I dreaming?"

Mary turned around, taking in the endless sea of sand, and shrugged. "Well if you are, I am too. No… I think this is real. I don't know how, but it is." She sighed. "God help us in this desert!"

"But…" Jean's voice faltered, and she took a deep breath before trying again. "But how did we end up here? It's not possible!"

Mary frowned, looking down at her feet while several thoughts swirled around her head. "You know, it's strange, but I was going to visit your brother originally – but for some reason I felt compelled to come to yours instead."

"What's that supposed to mean?" asked Jean, who was starting to panic now.

Just then George appeared in the doorway, looking first at his family and then at the sand dunes beyond. "What the... Mum? What's going on?"

Jean shrugged, looking more bewildered than he'd ever seen her look before. "That's what we're trying to figure out, George!" She was starting to sound slightly hysterical now. "We're lost... and I have no idea how we got here." She paused for a moment, thinking. "Did we go on holiday? Did I... forget?"

Mary laughed. "If we were on holiday, we wouldn't have brought the house with us, would we?" She looked pointedly at the building behind them. "No... this is something different..."

Jean shook her head. "It's just a dream, that's all. I'll wake up soon and everything will be back to normal... I'm sure..."

George didn't think his mum sounded sure at all, and he didn't blame her.

Lucy, of course, knew exactly what had happened – and how – but as she didn't want the fun to stop, she just sat down in the sand and started playing; if her mum knew she was the one who'd done this, she was bound to order Lucy to take them back, and she wanted to enjoy her little holiday for as long as possible.

"Mum," said George, who thought maybe he should try and take control of the situation, "the sand's getting in the house – maybe we should go inside and close the door while we try to figure this out?"

Jean nodded, following her son and her mother inside, while Lucy stayed where she was, playing with the sand – she was covering her feet and her legs, as though she were making half of her body disappear. She was having a great time.

Inside, George, Jean, and Mary sat down at the dining table, staring out of the windows at the sand surrounding the house. Mary's eyes were wide with wonder. "Isn't it amazing? Before, you could only see your neighbours' house from that window, and now we can see a lovely view of a desert. Just incredible!"

Jean, however, didn't think it was incredible at all – she was sitting with her head in her hands, muttering about how she needed to wake up and stop dreaming. George watched her with concern.

Placing his hand on her shoulder, George said quietly, "Don't say that, Mum. You're not dreaming – this is actually happening, and we need to come up with some sort of plan. We need a solution to get back home before we... I don't know... die of dehydration!"

Jean didn't move for a moment, trying to get herself under control, and when she looked up at George she said, "You're right, my son." She smiled. "Hey, you're the man of the house now."

Just then Lucy came bounding in, looking happier than all three of them put together. "Does this mean I don't need to go to school anymore?"

George shrugged as he looked out the window. "I don't think there *are* any schools around here."

Mary excused herself to go to the bathroom, and when Lucy went over to the kitchen sink to wash her hands, she found there was no water coming from the taps – none at all. "Mum, we don't have any water!" she cried.

Jean groaned. "Oh God, George – you're right. We're going to die of thirst in this desert!"

George patted her hand, trying to calm her down. "It's OK – we've got some bottles of water in the fridge. Those will last us for a while if we're careful."

Jean nodded. "Yes, yes, good. Don't use the water freely – we need to ration it!"

Smiling at his mother, George got up and headed over to the fridge, opening it to see how many bottles of water they had. "Oh no," he said as he looked inside, "the fridge isn't working either – all the food's going to go off." He sighed, thinking for a moment. "At least we have some cans in the cupboard, right? Beans, soup… that kind of thing."

Taking a deep breath, Jean went over to join her son in front of the fridge. "Yes we do. We'd better eat any food that will go off first – meats and things – and then any food that's sealed inside a container after that. What about the drinks?"

George counted. "Twelve bottles of water and a couple of cans of soda. I suppose we might be able to find water in other areas of the house… the toilet cistern, maybe?"

Suddenly, Jean thought of her mother. "George, run upstairs and warn your grandma not to flush the toilet, quick!"

George – followed quickly by Lucy – ran upstairs as fast as he could, and had just shouted, "Don't flush the toilet, Grandma!" when they heard the unmistakable sound of the toilet flushing.

Lucy sighed. "Oh, Grandma."

When the bathroom door opened and Mary stepped out, she raised her eyebrows, surprised to see Lucy and George waiting for her. "What's going on? You frightened me."

"We needed the water from the toilet cistern, that's why we came to tell you not to flush it," explained George. "Actually, I'm amazed it flushed at all – we've got no water in the house."

Mary lowered her head. "That's why it sounded so strange when I flushed it. I'm sorry, I didn't know," she replied helplessly.

Jean walked up the stairs then, smiling at her mother. "It's OK, we just need to be careful from now on. Everyone must go outside to do their private things, and we need to ration our food and water out as much as we can." She sat down on the top step of the stairs, staring at her family.

"But mum," whined Lucy, "how are we meant to go to the toilet outside? And how will we have a shower?"

"Oh darling," Jean said, shaking her head. "We won't be able to have any showers, I'm sorry." She sighed, looking up at the ceiling as she asked, "What sin have we committed to have ended up here?"

Mary sighed too. "I don't know, but it does seem as if God is punishing us for something."

There was silence for a few moments while everyone thought about this, and then Jean stood up, trying to take control of the situation. "Come on, let's all go and sit at the table – we need to come up with a plan, right now."

* * *

Once everyone had taken a seat at the dining room table, Jean started listing everything she knew about their current predicament. "So, we're somehow in the middle of the desert, with no water, no electricity, and no gas. That means the fridge isn't working, the lights aren't working, the radio isn't working, nor is the microwave or the TV..." She trailed off, sighing; they may as well have been transported back to the Stone Age.

Lucy became more and more miserable as she listened to her mother; if the TV wasn't working, that meant she wouldn't be able to watch *American Idol* anymore.

Jean carried on. "The cooker and the washing machine don't work either, so we really need to work as a team and rely on ourselves to get things done." Tears welled up in her eyes as she added, "That means we need to make our own food, wash our clothes by hand, and entertain ourselves without the help of machines. Do you think we can do that?"

She didn't sound very hopeful, George thought to himself, but he nodded in response. So did Lucy.

Mary moved her chair closer to Jean, taking her daughter in her arms as she replied, "Of course. Don't worry, I'm here, I'll help. And the kids will too. I'm sure it's only a matter of time before we find ourselves back home – by now the neighbours must have contacted the police and told them about our disappearance."

Jean wiped her eyes, nodded, and then stood up from the table. "Well, until then let's try and keep things as normal as we possibly can. It's time for breakfast." She smiled. "At least we have enough food for the next couple of days."

"Can we have some tea, Mum?" Lucy asked, her hopeful expression falling from her face when she heard her mum's reply.

"I'm afraid the kettle won't work without the electricity being on," Jean explained, "so if you want tea we'll have to collect wood – from somewhere, I don't know where – make a fire, and boil the water that way."

Lucy sighed. "I didn't think of that." It was amazing how much she relied on electricity every day, she thought to herself sadly.

With that, Jean started collecting things that would start going off sooner rather than later, putting milk and cereal on the table, along with the sausages and some bread. Everyone realised how hungry they were at the same time, and started tucking into the food with relish.

Just then, George thought of something – something he couldn't believe he hadn't thought of before – and taking his mobile phone out of his pocket, he turned it on and headed to his contacts list. It was only then that he saw the phone had no signal. The landline wasn't working either, and there was no internet to allow them to contact anyone online. They were completely cut off from the rest of the world.

Mary saw the look of disappointment on George's face, and smiling at her grandson, she said, "Try not to worry. Hopefully we'll start hearing the sound of police helicopters soon, coming to track us down – they'll see this house from the air no problem."

"But Grandma," George replied, frowning, "how will they know where to look for us? *We* don't even know where we are, so how could they? We don't even know what country we're in!"

Mary shrugged, still smiling as she replied, "We just need to have a little faith, that's all."

"Right," said Jean, who had started pacing up and down the room, "we should start exploring our area, see if we can find anyone else in this desert – maybe there'll be some surrounding villages we can get some water from."

Mary looked at her daughter, shocked. "And how exactly are we going to do that? We can't go out in this climate; it's far too hot!"

Jean stared back at her mother. "We're going to do what we need to do, no matter how hard that may be. The bottom line is, if we don't find another water source soon, we're all going to die of thirst!" She took a deep breath, trying to calm down.

"Look, Mum, I don't have the time or the patience to argue with you. George," she said, looking at her son, "go and get changed. We're leaving this house within the hour and we're not coming back until we've found at least some hint of civilisation out there, OK?"

George nodded, and Lucy ran over to her mother. "Can I come too?" she pleaded – she couldn't wait to get out there and explore.

"No," said Jean, "absolutely not. I need you to stay here with Grandma until we get back."

Lucy's face fell but she reluctantly agreed, and soon George and Jean were getting ready to head out into the sandy wilderness beyond the house. They were both wearing weather-appropriate outfits – loose clothing, big hats, and sunglasses – and they'd both absolutely covered themselves in sunscreen. Jean was holding an umbrella by her side.

"Why do you need an umbrella?" Lucy asked her mother. "Is it going to rain?"

Jean shook her head. "No, darling, this is to protect us from the sun so we don't get sunburnt." She turned to her son then, smiling as she said, "We'd better get going. Do you have enough food and water in your rucksack?"

"Yes Mum," George replied – they'd spent quite a few minutes discussing how they were going to ration out their supplies, and he'd taken as much as he'd dared.

Jean nodded and then turned to face her mother. "Look after Lucy please. Hopefully we'll be back in a few hours, and hopefully with more food and water."

Mary took her daughter's face in her hands, kissing her on the cheek. "If you happen to find a shop out there, bring us back some ice cream, will you?" She laughed, fanning her face with her hand.

"You got it," said Jean, smiling before heading over to the door. "Right, let's move."

Mary and Lucy watched George and Jean leave the house, and when they were gone, they went and sat down on the comfortable sofas in the lounge. It was going to be a long wait, that was for sure.

4

OUTSIDE, JEAN LOOKED OUT AT THE MOUNDS OF SAND. "Well, which way shall we go?"

"I really don't know," said George, not wanting to take on the responsibility of choosing their direction in case it was the wrong one.

Jean thought for a moment, then nodded. "OK, let's go behind the house – the ground seems a little flatter there; it should be easier to walk on the sand."

They started walking along together, trying to keep up a good pace so they could cover as much ground as possible, but soon it was clear that Jean was getting tired; she became short of breath and fell behind George.

"Are you OK, Mum?" he asked, looking over his shoulder.

"I'll be fine son," she replied, although it didn't sound very convincing. "Let's just keep going."

* * *

Back at the house, Lucy was getting tired too – tired of sitting around and doing nothing. "Grandma, is it OK if I go and play in the sand while I wait?" she asked. "There's a shovel in the garage that I could use to dig."

Mary thought about this for a moment. "OK, but make sure you wear a hat to protect your head from the sun, and don't wander too far from the house – if you do, your mum will be very cross with you. With me, too."

"It's OK," Lucy replied, "I'll just stay near the house. I'll be around the back."

After heading into the garage to grab the shovel, Lucy made her way to the back of the house, where there was at least some shade. Sitting in the shadow of the building, she started playing with the sand using her shovel, and after digging down about three feet, she realised the sand was getting wetter.

Curious, Lucy dug some more, watching in amazement as clear liquid started seeping through the sand. Jumping up, she ran back into the house, shouting, "Water! Grandma, I found water!"

Mary looked up from the magazine she'd been reading. "What do you mean? Bottles of water? Were they in the garage?"

"No," Lucy said, shaking her head, "under the sand outside! Come and have a look!"

Mary stared at her granddaughter as if she'd gone mad. "In the sand? Are you feeling OK? Perhaps you've got sunstroke…"

"No, I'm not sick and I'm not seeing things. Come, look for yourself!"

Rather reluctantly, Mary followed Lucy outside, heading around to the back of the house where Lucy had made her hole in the ground. Seeing the wet sand, Mary kneeled down, inspecting the liquid more closely. "You're right, Lucy!" she exclaimed happily, "There should be water here!"

Together, the two of them shovelled more sand from the pit, using their hands to dig when the bulky shovel started to become a nuisance. The more they dug, the more excited they got – this could be the thing that saved them!

* * *

A few hours later, Jean and George were still out, exploring the local area for any sign of life, but they'd found exactly nothing. Jean was exhausted, the sweat pouring freely down her face, and she kept lifting her water bottle to her forehead to try and cool herself down. Unfortunately, the water was now warm and it wasn't having any effect whatsoever.

"Mum," said George, his voice full of concern, "you're drinking too much water – we have to ration it, you know that." He took his rucksack off and peered into it. "We've only got one bottle left of the five we brought with us." He frowned at his mother, who was looking down at the ground. He didn't want to worry her more than she already was, but he had to make her see how important it was to save the water. At this rate, they wouldn't have enough for the journey back. And that was a worrying thought indeed.

Jean sighed. "I know, George, I know. Look… I don't think I'm going to make it. I don't have the strength or the energy to carry on in this hell." A tear slid down her cheek and she wiped it away absentmindedly. "I'm so sorry I brought you out here."

"You'll be fine!" George exclaimed, trying to calm her down. "We can only be about three or four miles from the house.

We'll rest a bit, gather our strength, and then start walking again. We'll make it, I promise."

Jean reluctantly agreed, and after sitting down on the sand for a few minutes to get their breath back, they carried on walking. Jean was so tired she could barely keep her eyes open, and after they'd been going for thirty minutes or so, George took her arm, half-carrying her back to the house.

"We're nearly there, Mum," George said a while later. "I can see the house!"

Jean smiled – although she was so tired it only came out as a vague half-smile – as she looked up at the house. There were two figures standing outside the back. "What are Lucy and Grandma doing outside the house?"

"I don't know," replied George, "but it sure is good to see them."

Jean agreed, but part of her wasn't happy to see them at all – not when she was coming back empty-handed. "I'm so embarrassed we didn't find anything," she whispered to George, and when they got to Lucy and Mary, Jean broke down crying. "I'm sorry," she said to her mother, "I failed. I can't even look after my own family..."

Mary took her daughter in her arms, giving her a hug as she stroked her hair. "Don't worry, Jean. We're going to be OK. Lucy found something."

Jean wiped her eyes before bending down and bringing Lucy into a hug. "What did you find, darling? Some more cans?"

"No," said Lucy, who kneeled down and pointed at a hole in the sand. "I dug a hole, and we found water!"

All tears suddenly gone, Jane peered down into the hole, gasping loudly when she saw it. "Oh God, water! Is it real? Perhaps it's a mirage… one of those desert hallucinations…"

Lucy laughed. "I don't know what a mirage is, but it's definitely real – look!" With that, Lucy scooped up some water in her hands and splashed it playfully on her mother's face.

Jean was so stunned that she just stood there for a moment, frozen on the spot, but when she reached up to her face and felt the water on her cheek, she burst out laughing. "It's real! You found water! Oh, you clever girl!" Then, kneeling down, she reached into the pit, bringing up handfuls of water that she splashed on her face. "George, come on, get in here! Wash your hands and your face – it feels so good!"

George walked over to the pit, copying his mother, and soon he felt cool enough to think properly again. "Come on, let's all go inside. We need to sit down."

The women followed him into his house, Jean shaking her head the whole time. "I can't believe we just went through hell to try and find water when there was some behind our house the whole time!"

As soon as they got into the lounge, Jean slumped down into a chair, absolutely exhausted. "I had no idea how difficult it would be to walk in the desert," she told Mary and Lucy. "I just thought it would be like walking on the streets in California, but the sun is just so *hot*-and the, sand keeps slipping under your feet…" She glanced over at her son. "George, if you hadn't been with me, I wouldn't have made it home. No question about it. Thank you, son."

George smiled at his mother before turning to Lucy. "I can't believe you found water – how did you do it?"

Lucy shrugged. "I wanted to play in the sand, and as soon as I dug down to a certain level, the water just started bubbling up!" She grinned widely. "I may not have been able to go out walking in the desert, but I *have* saved us from all dying of thirst!"

Jean smiled. "Yes, you have. Thank you Lucy. I have the best children in the world!"

Everyone rested for a while after the morning's exertions, and then Mary went into the kitchen to see what she could rustle up for lunch. Everyone sat down at the dining table, and after tucking into some fruit that would be going off in a couple of days, Jean looked up at her son. "I hate to say this, George, but I think we need to go out there again. We may have water now, but we still need food."

Mary put her apple down, gawping at her daughter as she asked, "Are you absolutely mad? You've just been saying how difficult it was, how awful it was! And you want to go out there *again?*"

Jean shook her head. "I don't *want* to, but I *have* to. We don't have any other choice! I'm physically drained, yes, but if I don't do something, we could starve to death!" She looked into the distance for a moment before shaking her head. "I won't let that happen, not to my family."

"But you're exhausted," Mary insisted. "You need to rest."

Jean thought about this for a moment, then nodded. "OK, we'll stay in for the rest of the day, but before sunrise tomorrow, I'm going to get up and leave the house. George, will you come with me?"

George reached out and briefly squeezed his mother's hand. "Of course I will."

"Thank you. We'll take one of the guns in case we come across anything – it's a good job your father taught you how to shoot; you shouldn't have any problems hunting."

Lucy, who had been staring at her mother as she came up with the plan, asked rather tentatively, "Can I come with you this time?"

"No, Lucy, I need you to stay at home with Grandma again."

"But I can help!" Lucy whined. "I helped today, didn't I?"

Jean smiled. "Yes you did – and I'm very grateful – but you helped by staying at home, so I need you to do the same tomorrow. Your help might be needed here, OK?"

Reluctantly, Lucy agreed, and the family finished their meagre meal. It was clear that everyone was still worried and tense about the whole situation, but with Lucy's discovery of the water under the sand, there was also something else surrounding the four of them as they ate: a sense of hope.

5

THE NEXT MORNING, JEAN WOKE UP TO THE SOUND OF HER alarm clock, which she'd set to go off before sunrise. The last thing she wanted to do was get out of bed – it was so dark and her body was so stiff from all the walking of the day before – and after sitting up for a moment, she lay back down again, exhausted.

George had heard the alarm clock from his room, and after getting out of bed, he walked down the corridor and knocked on his mother's bedroom door. "Mum?" he asked quietly, not wanting to wake Lucy and his grandmother.

"I'll be ready in a minute," she replied from inside, yawning loudly. "Could you pack some food and water? And don't forget the gun!"

"OK," George replied, before heading off to get everything together. He was tired too, but he knew they needed to find food – and fast. He was sitting at the dining table, waiting, when Jean finally appeared downstairs. By now it was almost dawn.

"Hurry up, Mum – before the sun rises and it starts getting really hot again."

Jean nodded, and the two of them rushed out the front door, stopping briefly to check their supplies.

"Which way shall we go this time?" George asked.

"We'll go the opposite way today," Jean replied, pointing in front of her, "maybe we'll have better luck than yesterday."

George agreed and soon they were off again, trying to ignore their aching muscles, which were painful from all the physical activity of the day before.

At least getting out before the sun had risen meant they had a while before it got really hot, and after a couple of hours of walking at a moderate pace, they got to a big hill made of stone and sand.

"Let's get to the top and look around," George suggested, and holding his mother's arm to help her, they both walked up the hill.

When they got to the top, Jean gasped. Over the crest of the hill, where she'd expected to see more endless desert, there was a beautiful, lush, green oasis.

George was so happy to see this sight that he ran down the other side of the hill, straight over to a small lake, which he jumped into and started splashing around. The water felt cool and clean and wonderful.

A minute later Jean joined him, peering down into the water. "This is amazing – do you think the water's drinkable?"

"Of course it's drinkable!" George replied happily. "It's from a fresh spring!"

Jean laughed. "Well, it *was* fresh until you jumped into it!"

George was just about to reply when he froze, looking at something in the distance. When he did speak, he lowered his voice to a whisper. "Look, Mum – there are deer over there! I think they might be waiting for us to leave so they can come and drink the water."

"Deer?" Jean whispered, turning around to look at them. "George – this is the perfect opportunity; we can hunt one of them and be able to eat for another couple of days!" She paused, thinking for a moment. "OK, we need to go and hide somewhere and then wait while they drink. When they're about to leave, you can shoot one of them."

George had never hunted an animal before, but he knew how much trouble his family would be in if they didn't get more food soon, so he agreed with his mother's plan before wading out of the spring.

They hid behind a small hill of sand, where George could prepare his gun out of sight of the deer, and then waited as they walked over to the spring. With sweat pouring down his face as if it were raining on him, George set up the gun, aiming it at the herd of deer as they bent down to drink from the spring.

"Get ready," whispered Jean, but George was anything but ready. He could barely see where he was pointing his gun thanks to the sweat running into his eyes, and both his hands were shaking violently.

Realising how nervous her son was, Jean moved a little closer. "Relax, George, it'll be fine. I know that you love animals – I do too – but now is not the time to be sensitive. We're hungry, we need food, and if we don't get any, we'll die. It's as simple as that. I don't want us to go to bed hungry tonight, do you?"

George shook his head. "No, I don't," he replied, and after taking a deep breath and wiping the sweat from his face, he aimed the gun again. This time, his hands were steady. He counted to three in his head, took another deep breath, and pulled the trigger. The sound reverberated around the area, scattering the herd of deer as they rushed to get away from the loud noise – all but one. George had hit one of them right in the head, and it had fallen instantly to the ground, dead.

"Good shot!" shouted Jean happily, and George nodded in response.

In truth, he was still a bit shaken by the whole thing. At least it had died straight away, he told himself – it wouldn't have felt much pain.

George and Jean ran over to the body of the deer, and after making sure it was actually dead, George took some rope out of his backpack – he'd found it in the garage the night before and had thought it might come in handy. With some help from his mum, he tied the rope around the deer's neck and front legs, making sure it was secure before dragging it away from the spring.

Jean took the gun from George while he took charge of the deer, and as they walked away from the oasis, George made a mental note to bring the sledge from the garage next time too – it would be much, much easier to carry any animals back with that.

As they walked, George kept looking around them, feeling rather uneasy. "I hope hunting isn't forbidden here," he commented, also hoping that no one had seen him shoot the deer.

"Don't worry about that," Jean said. "We haven't come across any other people, have we? And anyway, if it *is* forbidden, I'll deal with it."

They carried on walking, and when they were about a mile away from the oasis, they started to hear some rather strange noises coming from the distance. They paused to listen, looking around, and a few moments later they saw six wild dogs behind them – they'd obviously been following their trail, smelling the blood from the deer as George dragged it along the sand.

"Mum," George said, panicking, "I think those dogs might attack us to get the deer – what shall we do?"

By now the dogs were prowling closer and closer, spreading out from each other as though planning to surround George and Jean.

"Oh, George," Jean replied, her voice shaking. "I don't know!"

"Give me the gun," he replied. "At least we're armed."

"No!" Jean shouted loudly, making George jump. "If you shoot at them and end up wounding some of them, they'll just get more vicious and will attack us straight away!"

"Then what shall we do?" George asked again, completely out of ideas. As the dogs got closer and closer, he could feel the fear building up inside him.

By now they were just feet away, and George and Jean leaped back as two of the wild dogs pounced on the deer, pulling it towards them and the rest of the dogs. The whole pack then got stuck in, eating the deer right in front of them, their sharp teeth soon ripping into the flesh.

George and Jean were now covered in sweat, both from the heat and from nerves, and shaking, Jean grabbed her son's sleeve, pulling him back away from the dogs. "Don't worry, darling – we'll just have to come back and hunt another day. At least we know where to go now, and besides, if we hadn't had that deer, those dogs would have definitely attacked us.

God helped us get the deer for that very reason. Come on, let's go."

George knew his mother was right, but it still hurt to leave the deer behind. He'd hated to kill it, but part of him had felt proud that he'd got it on his first go, and even prouder that he was stepping up as the man of the house, providing for his family. Now, he felt as if he'd failed them completely.

Disappointed and angry, the two of them walked back home, tired and broken.

* * *

Lucy was just attaching some balloons with long strings to a desert bush when she saw her mother and brother appear in the distance. She waited while they walked over, and when they got close to the house, she ran over to them, peering up to look at their faces. "Did you get anything?" she asked eagerly.

George said nothing, not even glancing at his sister as he walked past her and into the house, but Jean kneeled down and brought Lucy in for a cuddle. "I'll tell you the whole story inside. Now promise me you'll stay in – as we've just discovered, it's dangerous outside."

Intrigued, Lucy promised, and soon they were all sitting at the dining table.

Mary had put some fruit juice and biscuits on the table, and everyone was eating and drinking very slowly, as if that would somehow make the meal seem bigger than it actually was.

Jean ate slowest of all; she was slumped in her chair, still short of breath, absolutely exhausted from the day's events. And it wasn't just the walking that had tired her out – the appearance of the wild dogs had shaken her up badly; now she had even more things to worry about.

"Are you OK?" Mary asked, frowning. "I told you not to go out again in this heat!"

"I'll be alright," Jean insisted, before turning to face George. "I'm too tired to tell the story – can you do it?"

George nodded, and ten minutes later, Mary and Lucy had heard all about the hill, the oasis, the deer, and the wild dogs. Mary shook her head every so often while she listened, whereas Lucy found the whole thing fascinating.

"We're lucky we had that deer," Jean added, "otherwise the dogs probably would have eaten us!"

Lucy's eyes widened at this – could dogs really eat people? The thought made her shiver.

It was then that Jean started crying, all the fear and frustration of the day finally spilling out of her. "I've never been so frightened in my entire life. All the time I kept thinking: if I didn't get home, who would look after the family?"

"Thank you for thinking of us," said Mary kindly, "but don't worry about coming back empty-handed; we're just glad you came back alive. That's the most important thing. And we're not completely out of food – we still have beans, tuna, and bread to eat. I'm sure it'll tide us over until the police get here."

George nodded. "And we can try again tomorrow to get another deer. Like you said, now we know where to go, it'll be much easier."

Jean sighed as she stared sadly at her son. "George, I'm sorry, but I don't think I can go hunting with you tomorrow. I'm not feeling well… I'm not sure I'll have the strength."

"It doesn't matter, Mum, I can go by myself. Don't worry about me." George sat up straight in his seat, trying to show no fear. After all, he was the man of the house now.

"I'll come with you, George!" exclaimed Lucy, determined to go along on at least one trip into the desert.

"No," snapped Jean, before George even had a chance to reply, "it's not safe for you. The desert is too dangerous, especially now we know those wild dogs are nearby. It's not just the heat you have to worry about – there are plenty of vicious animals out there that could harm you."

"But Mum," Lucy replied, going into whining mode, "I'm much faster than you – I can run if anything comes after me. And anyway, someone has to go with George. What if something happens to him? We'll need a second person to come back and report it."

Mary raised her eyebrows, surprised at how mature her granddaughter sounded all of a sudden. "While I hope nothing like that ever happens, I think Lucy might be right. Two people have got to be better than one."

Reluctantly, Jean agreed. "I suppose you're right. I'll see how I feel in the morning; we can discuss it again then."

* * *

The next day, George woke up to find Mary leaning over his bed. "I was just about to wake you," she said. "It's time to get up and go hunting again, if you're up to it."

Still a bit groggy from sleep, George slowly sat up as he rubbed his eyes. "Is Mum feeling better then?" he asked.

"No," said Mary. "She's up and in the kitchen, but she's not going to go with you. You'll have to take Lucy."

Surprised, George climbed out of bed, wanting to hear this directly from his mum. "OK Grandma, thanks. I'll be there in a few minutes." Once Mary had left he got changed, before washing his hands and face in a bucket of water they'd filled up from the pit outside. Finally, he retrieved his shotgun from the cabinet before heading downstairs.

"Mum? Are you sure about this? About Lucy going, I mean?"

Jean was sitting at the table, her face pale. "Yes. I wish I felt well enough to come with you, but I don't think I'd get more than ten feet from the house before collapsing." She stood up and walked over to George, taking his hands in hers. "Promise me you'll look after your little sister. I couldn't bear it if anything happened to either of you."

George stared back into his mother's eyes – her wide, frightened eyes – and smiled. "I promise. We'll be fine."

"George, I'm coming with you!" shouted Lucy as she bounded into the room, full of energy. "Are we going now?"

George couldn't help but laugh. "You must be mad, actually *wanting* to come. Are you sure about this?"

Lucy nodded enthusiastically. "Oh yes, I can't let my brother go out there all alone and get torn to pieces by the wild animals. Also, I'm fed up of staying in the house and doing boring chores. I want to go out and explore!"

"OK, OK," George said, holding his hand up to stop Lucy from talking. "Don't give me a headache before we even leave."

"I won't," Lucy replied, "but I thought you'd like to know that I found the sledge in the garage and put it outside, so we can bring back whatever we hunt more easily."

George was impressed, but all he said in response was, "You mean whatever *I* hunt. You'll be doing nothing of the sort."

Lucy nodded, this time a little less enthusiastically. "So when are we going?"

"Now, if you're ready," George responded, before saying goodbye to his mother and grandmother.

Jean and Mary kissed him on the cheek, then brought Lucy in for a big hug between the two of them.

"You be careful," Jean told Lucy. "I hope you succeed."

"I'm sure we will," Lucy replied confidently, making Jean and Mary laugh.

Moments later, George and Lucy were walking away from the house in the direction of the oasis, setting a good pace. The sun hadn't yet reached its peak in the sky, but soon it began to get hotter and hotter. In fact, it was hotter than Lucy ever would have imagined it could be, and she made sure to keep sipping water from her bottle every so often so she wouldn't start feeling dizzy.

By now Lucy was sweating profusely, and feeling more than a little tired, but she was determined to keep up with the pace set by her brother – she didn't want to give him an excuse not to take her again. She wanted to prove to him that she could do this.

At long last they got to the oasis, Lucy's eyes widening as she took in all the lush vegetation in front of her. "This is amazing!" she exclaimed. "Well worth the walk!"

George smiled as he led her over to the spring, where they washed their faces and filled up their water bottles. "Now," he said, once they'd quenched their thirst, "you can see a herd of deer over there." He pointed at the animals, which were standing in more or less the same place as they had been the day before. "We'll go and hide, and when they come to drink from the stream, I'll try and shoot one. OK?" He was a bit worried at how Lucy would react to seeing a deer get killed, but – at the moment, at least – she seemed remarkably calm.

The two of them went and hid behind the sand hill, and just as before, after a while the deer came and started drinking from the spring. George set up his shotgun – this time without his hands shaking at all – and took aim, shooting one of the deer in the neck and causing the others to run away as fast as their legs could carry them.

George ran over to check the deer was dead, while Lucy dragged the sledge out from behind the hill. She helped her brother get the body onto the sledge, then both of them stood back, looking down at the majestic creature.

"Are you OK, Lucy?" George asked.

She thought about this for a while before smiling at her brother. "Yes. It's sad, but it would be more sad for us to die of hunger."

George had to laugh at that; his sister sure had a way with words. "Right, I think we'll tie the gun to the sledge and then we can both pull it together, how does that sound?"

"That's not a bad idea," she said, and once George had tied the gun on with the rope, they both started pulling the sledge back in the direction of the house.

George had remained relatively calm for the journey so far, but now he was starting to get anxious, glancing around every few steps to see if the wild dogs were going to appear. Then, after they'd been walking for about a mile, he heard them.

Turning to his sister, he said frantically, "Lucy, the dogs are here! If they get close, we're going to have to give them the deer and then run away as fast as we can – otherwise, they'll attack us too. Do you understand?"

Lucy, however, didn't understand. "How can you say that?" she asked angrily. "How can you just leave the deer behind when Mum and Grandma are at home, waiting for us to get food? We'll starve! We have a gun and Dad says you're a good shot, so why don't you shoot at them and frighten them off?"

George shook his head, trying to get himself under control; he was clearly very, very scared. "Yeah I'm a good shot, but these dogs could-"

"If you won't shoot them," Lucy interrupted, "give me the gun and I'll do it!"

George didn't know what to say; he was terrified of the dogs and more than a little surprised that his sister – who was much younger than him – was apparently taking control of the situation. He watched as she bent down and started undoing the rope that tied the gun to the sledge, his mind in a whirl, but when she stood back up with the gun in her hands, he suddenly came to his senses.

Taking the shotgun from Lucy, George aimed it at the approaching dogs and started firing. His hands were shaking and he missed the first time, but on the second go he shot one of the animals in the head, causing the others to howl and scatter. They ran away in several different directions, and George breathed a huge sigh of relief as he watched them go. "I did it!" he exclaimed, the adrenaline now pumping through his body and filling him with energy. "I made them run away!"

"You see," said Lucy, smiling, "that wasn't so hard, was it?" She turned to the dogs, shouting after them, "Better luck next time!"

George laughed, then patted his little sister on the back before strapping the gun onto the sledge again. Happy now, the two of them carried on walking, carrying their deer behind them.

* * *

Back at the house, Jean had been keeping busy while her kids were gone; she was so worried about them, and she needed something to distract her thoughts while she waited for them to get back. So, she'd dug deeper into Lucy's pit in the sand, and had collected more water for the house in any container she could find – bottles, buckets, cups, mugs… the lot.

She was standing in the pit – which was now more than a metre deep – when she heard a noise coming from some-where nearby; it sounded a little like the wild dogs had the day before, but not quite.

Scrambling out of the hole as quickly as she could, she looked around to see a hyena heading towards her, and leaving the bucket of water behind, she ran into the house, screaming at Mary as she went, "Mum, Mum! Close all the doors and windows! There's a hyena out here!"

"Oh God," Mary replied, shutting the open windows in the kitchen, "that's all we need, another wild animal prowling around outside the house! I do hope George and Lucy can get back safely."

"So do I," said Jean, looking out of the window anxiously, but luckily she didn't have to wait too long before Lucy and George rushed in through the front door, pulling the sledge behind them.

"You're OK!" shouted Mary, running over and hugging them both. "Did you see the hyena out there?"

George and Lucy exchanged a look of confusion. "No," replied Lucy, "but we did get a deer! Guess who's getting a good dinner tonight!"

Jean rushed over then, glancing briefly at the deer before pulling both of her children in for a big hug. "I'm so glad you made it back OK," she replied, "and the deer is just wonderful! We don't need to have beans again tonight!"

After detangling himself from his mother's arms, George took the deer into the garage, while the rest of the family sat down at the dining table.

"Did you have any problems?" asked Jean.

"No Mum," Lucy replied, smiling, "no problems at all!"

Jean frowned, unsure whether to believe her or not, but the next moment George came back into the room, saying proudly, "I shot one of the wild dogs today!"

Jean gasped. "They attacked you again? What happened?" She looked angrily at Lucy. "And this time I want the truth!"

Lucy sighed. She hadn't wanted to lie; she just didn't want to scare her mother. "Don't worry, Mum," she said, shooting her brother a glance, "we scared them away with some gunshots. They didn't even get close – we weren't in danger."

Jean looked from her daughter to her son, but George said nothing.

"And you didn't see the hyena?" she asked. "I think he was coming to get a drink from our pit."

"No," George replied, thankful he could be truthful on this point at least. "We didn't see it at all; it's probably gone by now."

Jean nodded. "Well, just keep a lookout, OK? You have to be very careful from now on, whenever you go out – even if it's just outside the house."

The two kids agreed, and Jean sat back in her chair, sighing. She felt exhausted again, and she wasn't even the one who'd walked to the oasis and back!

6

AFTER EVERYONE HAD RESTED FOR A FEW HOURS, JEAN, Mary, and George headed into the garage, taking the deer outside – after checking there were no wild dogs or hyenas around – before also bringing out the big family barbecue they sometimes used in the summer.

Between them they figured out how to prepare the deer, and after successfully lighting the barbecue, they started cooking the meat. It smelled delicious, and all four of them were excited at the prospect of eating something fresh after all the tinned food and biscuits they'd been living off.

Once the meat was done they took everything back inside, sitting at the dining table to eat, and for the first time in a couple of days, everyone seemed pretty cheerful as they ate. It was amazing what a good meal could do to a person's outlook, thought George as he looked around the table at his family. He was glad he'd been able to kill the deer, and even more glad that Lucy had convinced him to scare away the dogs. He had to start giving his little sister some credit.

They all went to bed with full stomachs that night, and the next day, Lucy felt happy as she got up early to go and get more water from the pit.

Her good mood, however, vanished when she saw what was waiting for her outside: the hyena. Rushing back into the house, she shut the door before shouting out, "You were right, Mum, we have a guest out there!"

"Thank God," replied Mary as she appeared in the doorway of the kitchen. "At last someone's come to visit us! Is it a man or a woman?"

Lucy smiled sheepishly. "Sorry, Grandma – I meant the hyena. There's no person out there."

Mary's face fell at that, but she quickly got back to her usual cheerful demeanour. "Well, in that case, maybe we'd better give the hyena something to eat; he might leave us alone then."

They both walked into the kitchen, and Jean, who had heard everything, stood up from the table. "Don't be silly! If we give him anything to eat, he'll just keep coming back; he'll never leave us alone!"

Lucy nodded. "Like that stray cat who kept coming to the house! We should try and frighten him instead. Or maybe something a little worse…"

"Frighten who?" asked George, who'd just come downstairs. "What are you talking about?"

"The hyena's back," Lucy told her brother, "he's out there right now. Can you go and destroy him, or do you want me to go?"

George shook his head; Lucy was growing up far too quickly for his liking. "I'll get the gun," he said, leaving the room as his mother shouted after him, "Be careful, George!"

After getting the shotgun, George headed down the hallway, carefully opening the door to make sure the hyena wasn't going to run straight inside. He could see it standing a few feet away from the house, and stepping through the door, he fired the gun into the air, making the hyena run off in fright.

At the sound of the gun Lucy ran out, looking around wildly. "Where's the carcass?" she asked. "Didn't you kill him?"

"No," replied George, "I just scared him away."

Lucy didn't look too happy. "You should have killed him," she insisted. "*I* would have. What if it comes back tomorrow? What if someone goes to get water and gets injured or killed? You'll be responsible!" Her face red with anger, she stomped back into the house, leaving her brother standing outside, dumbfounded. Since when had his little sister changed so much?

A few moments later he followed her inside, walking into the kitchen.

"What happened, George?" his mum asked, frowning. "We heard a gunshot."

"I scared the hyena off; I don't think he'll come back again."

Lucy sighed. "We shall see."

Thinking she'd better step in to stop a potential argument from happening, Jean said, "We need to collect some more wood and brambles to make a fire. Can you go and find some please?"

Together, Lucy and George replied, "Yes, Mum."

"Good, thank you. Me and your grandmother will do the housework until you come back."

After retrieving the sledge from the garage, George and Lucy headed out into the desert, and within a few hours the sledge was full of wood, brambles, and dry plants they could burn for the fire. Taking their load back to the house, they headed out again, slowly filling the sledge a second time.

George was just trying to pull out a plant from the roots when he realised the branches were moving, and even though he retreated as fast as he could, he didn't step back quite quick enough; slithering out from under the plant, a large snake bit him on the leg.

George shouted out before falling to the ground in pain. "Lucy," he managed to gasp, "get away from that snake!"

Lucy, however, had other ideas; she was staring at it intently as it slithered around her. She recognised it from the snake book her grandmother had given her, and from watching thte inernet, and was relieved to realise it was one of the non-poisonous ones. Of course, George didn't know that, and Lucy decided she'd have a little fun with her brother – after all, she was still annoyed that he'd let the hyena get away.

"What's the matter?" she asked George as the snake slithered away.

"It bit me!" he screamed. "I don't know what to do!" He was panicking, clutching his leg as though it were about to fall off.

Lucy stared at him for a moment. "I don't want to scare you, George," she said, "but if you don't get any treatment soon, you could die. In a very horrific way."

"Oh God!" George moaned.

Trying to hide a smile, Lucy continued. "We need to get home as soon as possible." Then, taking the gun from George's hand, the two of them started walking off in the direction of the house, George hopping on one foot while he pulled the half-full sledge behind him.

It didn't take them long to get back, and as soon as they got to the door, Lucy and George rushed inside.

"Mum!" yelled George, "I've been bitten by a snake!"

Jean and Mary appeared in the corridor. "What did you say?" Jean asked, her face turning pale.

"When we were collecting plants, a snake came out of nowhere and bit me on the leg!" George explained, still frantic.

Jean – if possible – went even paler, before taking her son by the arm. "Come on, lie down on the sofa in the lounge. We need to check your leg."

While they headed into the lounge, Mary went and retrieved the first aid kit from the kitchen, and soon she was cleaning out the wound and tying it up with some bandages. "I'm afraid that's all I can do," she said once she'd finished, "I know nothing about how to treat a snake bite – do you?" she asked Jean.

Jean shook her head, trying to think. "No… I've never known anyone who was bitten… I have no idea!"

Mary sat down, staring into the distance for a moment. After a while she said, "The only thing I can remember is that if someone's bitten by a snake, you need to act quickly before the venom reaches the heart."

"Act quickly?" asked George, who was starting to feel very sick indeed. "What does that mean?"

Mary glanced sympathetically at George as she whispered, "If someone's been bitten on the leg, well, it means… cutting off the leg to stop the venom spreading."

"No!" George yelled, sitting up and clutching his leg. "You can't do that! I can't lose my leg! How am I meant to go hunting without my leg? And what about school? How am I going to play football? How am I going to do *anything*?!"

Jean buried her face in her hands, shaking her head as she tried to think. This was awful, it was just awful. Lucy, on the other hand, was sitting at the bottom of the stairs, watching what was going on through the doorway to the lounge, looking at her brother. He was lying back down again, panicking, absolutely convinced he was going to die.

Mary, who was sitting next to her grandson, took a tissue from her pocket and wiped the sweat from George's forehead. Turning to face Jean, her expression one of utter sadness, she whispered, "We need to act quickly, before it's too late. I'll leave the decision to you."

By now Jean's entire body was shaking, and after considering the options for what felt like forever – but was in fact only a minute or so – she stood up, her decision made. "We need to get him on the dining table," she said, and without saying a word in response, Mary helped her daughter carry George to the table. He was only semi-conscious and didn't know what was happening.

"Stay with him while I go to the garage," Jean told her mother, and when she came back she was holding a saw. It was wooden, the only one she could find. With tears running down her cheeks, Jean said, "Mum, please cover his eyes; if he wakes up, I don't want him to see this. I just wish we had some way of numbing the pain for him."

Nodding, Mary grabbed a piece of cloth from the counter, and was just about to drape it over George's eyes when he came around, ripping the cloth out of her hands as he asked, "What are you doing?" His gaze moved over to his mother, and when he saw her terrified expression and the wooden saw in her hand, he started flailing around on the table. Terror was ripping through his body, filling up every single part of him, and as bile rose into his mouth, he begged his mum to stop. "No! What are you doing? Please don't do this, *please don't do this!*"

"I'm sorry, George," Jean replied, the tears now streaming down her face faster than she could wipe them away, "I have to do it. I have to do it to save your life!"

With a strength he didn't know she had, Mary held George's head in position on the table so he couldn't look down at his legs, and with her hands shaking, Jean put the saw into position, hovering above George's knee. She was just about to start cutting into the flesh when Lucy screamed, "Stop it! Mum, stop that right now!"

Jean turned to look at her daughter. "I'm sorry, Lucy, I know this is hard, but I have to do it. Why don't you go to your room, so you don't have to see it?" With that she turned back to George and got the saw in position again.

"No!" Lucy screamed, much louder this time. "The snake that bit George wasn't poisonous – I know from my book! It's just a wound; it'll get better soon."

Upon hearing this, the three of them were stunned into silence for several seconds.

"Did you just say," asked Jean, her voice shaking, "that this snake wasn't poisonous?"

"Yes, it's harmless," Lucy explained, "George is going to be fine."

"How can you be sure?" Jean asked, frowning as though trying to figure out if she should believe her daughter or not.

Lucy shrugged. "I've read about it, and I've seen them at the zoo. I know all about different types of snakes; I did a project on them for school."

"She does like all those reptile books," Mary said.

George, who had been listening very carefully to every word his sister said, and who had realised that he wasn't feeling as much pain as he thought he had been, suddenly leaped off the table and started running at Lucy. "I'm going to kill you!" he screamed as she ran upstairs and locked herself in her room.

Jean collapsed onto a nearby chair, tears still streaming down her face, her mouth wide open. "Did you see what I nearly did?" she asked her mother after a while. "I nearly cut off my son's leg! What's happening to us? What's *wrong* with me?"

Mary sat down next to her, scooting her chair over so she could reach out and hold her daughter's hand. "You were going to do what you thought you *had* to do to save your son's life. There's no shame in that." She shook her head, sighing. "Thank God we didn't have to do it."

Jean nodded slowly. "Thank God." She frowned. Lucy? "But what about Isn't she acting strange?"

That night, after an extremely quiet dinner during which no one said a word to anyone else, everyone went to bed early. It was a day they would all rather pretend hadn't happened at all.

* * *

The next morning, Jean woke everyone up bright and early. "Come on," she told her family as she dragged each of them out of bed, "we're all going to the oasis to have a proper wash. It's about time."

Once everyone was up and had eaten their breakfast of left-over cereal, they started gathering supplies for their journey: shampoo, soap, and anything else they thought they'd need in order to have a good bath. Lucy went to the garage to retrieve the sledge, and as she was poking around in some of the boxes in the corner, she came across some fireworks.

After loading everything onto the sledge – including fresh clothes, food, and the shotgun should they run into any trouble – and securing it all with the rope, the four of them headed off into the desert in the direction of the oasis. It was nice to be going with the whole family, thought George, even though he hadn't exactly forgiven his sister for the snake prank, and Lucy was thinking the same thing; she was holding hands with her grandma while they walked, as if they were just out for a normal, everyday stroll.

When they got to the spring in the oasis, Mary – who was the only one who hadn't seen it before – gasped in delight. "What a beautiful place! If only it were closer to the house so we wouldn't have to walk so far to get here."

They started washing their hands and faces, and Jean ordered everyone to have a full bath to get as clean as possible. "After all," she added, "we don't know when we'll next all be back here."

The four of them had a wonderful time, bathing in the spring and then getting changed into lovely fresh clothes – it was amazing how much a good clean could help with your outlook – and soon they were heading back to the house, all of them in much higher spirits than before.

Unfortunately, their good moods didn't last too long, as a couple of miles into their walk, George noticed they were being followed by the wild dogs. Not wanting to worry anyone, he didn't mention them to his family, but he did get the shotgun ready in case he'd have to use it.

Just then the dogs started barking, making Jean jump. "Oh no, not those wild dogs again!" she exclaimed. "We don't even have a deer we can give to them this time!"

"Don't worry," said Lucy rather confidently, "they won't bother us."

Mary turned to look, squinting her eyes so she could get a better view of them. "Are you sure they're as dangerous as you say they are? They don't look very big to me."

Just then, however, the dogs ran towards the family, and when they started surrounding them, Lucy glanced at George. "Well, what are you waiting for?" she asked him. "If you won't kill them, at least point your gun at the sky and fire to scare them away!"

George did as Lucy suggested, and after shooting upwards two times, the dogs retreated about twenty metres. The family started walking again, but it didn't take long for the dogs to come back – they were obviously so hungry that the gun wasn't enough to deter them for long. This time they started barking loudly, snapping in their direction, and Jean – who was frozen to the spot in fear – grabbed Lucy's hand in her left and Mary's in her right.

George started shooting again, but even though he knew he had plenty of bullets left, the gun stopped firing. "Mum!" George yelled. "I think the bullet got stuck; it's not working! We're going to have to physically defend ourselves!"

"Great, that's all we need," Jean replied sarcastically, but her shaky voice betrayed the fear she was feeling.

By now the dogs were so close they were nearly on top of the family, and one of them jumped up at Mary's leg, almost biting her. "Get away!" she shouted at it, "Leave us the hell alone!" Turning the shotgun around, George brought it down on top of the dog, which stunned it for a moment but that was about it – a second later, the dog tried to bite him too.

Jean and Mary were crying now, holding each other tightly and muttering words under their breath – George thought they were both praying to God. He looked on, frustrated that he couldn't help.

What on earth was going to become of them?

Just then, Lucy remembered the fireworks she'd brought with her from the garage, and bending down, she took one from the sledge, lighting it with the barbecue lighter she'd found in the kitchen drawer. Holding it out, she threw it at the dogs, where it exploded over them, the loud bang and the sparks scaring the wild dogs and making them run away.

The loud bang had made everyone jump, but the resulting smoke from the firework – which was thick and which covered everything in a grey haze – meant that Mary and Jean had no idea what had just happened.

"What's going on?" asked Jean, sounding scared. "What was that?"

"Have they gone?" asked Mary, coughing as the smoke entered her mouth.

As the smoke gradually started to clear, George looked at his sister in wonder. "Where did you find that?" he asked, his voice full of pride. He was clearly impressed.

"Where did she find what?" asked Jean, who could now see the rest of her family again, the smoke having dissipated into the air.

"Lucy found some fireworks – she threw one at the dogs and made them run away," said George, smiling at his sister.

"Oh, well done!" exclaimed Jean, going over to hug her daughter. "That was very clever of you!" After kissing her on the cheek, she turned to face George. "As for you, I think you'd better remember to clean your guns properly."

George's face fell; he knew he'd let everyone down.

"But thank you for trying to save us," added Jean, "that was very brave."

George smiled, although his heart wasn't really in it, and soon the family were heading back towards the house.

"Do you know," Mary said as they walked, "I was so frightened back there I think I wet myself! I need to go back to the spring and wash myself again!"

Everyone laughed at this, and after some discussion, they all headed back towards the spring; they didn't think the dogs would come after them again today, but Lucy kept her eye on the remaining fireworks, just in case.

7

THE NEXT FEW DAYS CARRIED ON AS NORMAL, WITH THE family getting water from the pit and using up the rest of their food supplies, and one morning Jean suggested they all go to the spring again to have another proper bath.

Everyone agreed enthusiastically, wanting to get clean, and they made the journey to the oasis together, looking out for the wild dogs the whole way.

The spring was lovely and refreshing as usual, but as they were washing themselves they started to realise that the wind was picking up. It got stronger and stronger, and by the time they'd finished bathing, it had developed into a full-on sandstorm.

"Quick!" Jean yelled over the sound of the wind, "Put your clothes in your bags or they'll get ruined!"

All four of them worked together to pack everything away, and by the time they were done, the sky had turned an alarming shade of red as the sand swirled all around them.

"We need to get back to the house, as soon as possible!" Jean ordered.

"But Mum," said George, looking around him in a panic, "we won't be able to find our way back in this storm! Who knows where we'll end up?"

"Well what shall we do then?" Jean asked, exasperated.

George pointed to a nearby hill. "There's a cave up there, I saw it the other day. Hopefully it'll be big enough for us to hide in until the storm passes."

"Sounds good to me," said Mary, who wanted very much to get out of that awful wind, "as long as there aren't any wild animals in there!"

That thought scared Jean, but with no other options and with the wind picking up even more, the four of them headed over to the hill, walking up to the cave – it was pretty hard going with the sand coming at them from all sides, but they managed to make it there without too many stumbles and falls.

"Here," said George as they got to the mouth of the cave, "get in. It looks pretty safe and secure."

"And dark too," said Mary as they made their way inside. "I can hardly see anything!" There was a hint of panic in her voice, and Jean took her hand.

"Don't worry, Mum," she said, trying to soothe her, "the storm will be over soon – we'll be back at the house before you know it."

"I hope so," replied Lucy, who was in a bit of a huff. She'd been having a great time in the spring, and now she was all covered in sand again.

The four of them sat down on the ground, near to the mouth of the cave so they could peer out but not so near they got covered in sand every time a strong wind blew past.

No one knew how long they sat there for, but it must have been hours going from how sore their bodies felt from sitting on the cold cave ground for so long, and still the storm raged outside, the oasis now partially covered in sand from the desert. There was hardly a speck of green left to be seen.

"Mum," George said eventually, "I think we might have to spend the night here in the cave; it looks like it's getting dark."

Jean nodded. "I hate to agree, but I don't think there's anything else we can do. Right, let's take out all the blankets and towels we brought with us — we should be able to make some temporary beds out of them for tonight."

Lucy moaned in the semi-darkness. "So after spending all that time washing ourselves, we've now got to spend the night in this dirty cave?"

"Don't start whining," Jean warned her.

"Oh, let her whine!" Mary snapped. "I'm not very happy about this either, you know. It took me so long to wash my hair, and now it's just a mess again! You know how difficult it is for me to come all the way here."

"I know," Jean said, in a quieter voice this time. "Let's just try and get some sleep. I'm sure everything will seem better in the morning."

Everyone was so exhausted they didn't argue, and although they tried to get as much sleep as possible, that was much easier said than done.

By the morning, everyone was more than a little grumpy.

"I was so cold last night!" Mary exclaimed.

"My back hurts," whined Lucy.

"To be honest, I didn't get any sleep at all," Jean said, sighing.

"Well, at least there weren't any wild animals stuck in here with us!" George said, trying to lighten the mood. Going by the unimpressed looks on his family's faces, however, he didn't succeed.

"Come on," said Jean, "we'd better start walking before the sun gets any stronger."

They headed towards the cave mouth, halting when they saw the sand – it was blocking half of the entrance. Jean poked her head out the bit that wasn't blocked with sand, and was shocked to see that the trees were all half-covered in sand too. It was just everywhere.

"Oh, I do hope we can find our way back home OK," Mary said.

"Don't worry, Grandma," George said, doing his best to comfort her, "we're going to make it."

The four of them worked together to push the sand out of the mouth of the cave, and soon they were walking back in what they hoped was the direction of the house. The sand-storm had completely changed their environment, however, and everything looked completely different. There were hills where there hadn't been hills before, and where they expected to see mounds of sand, there was just flat desert. It was all extremely confusing.

After a while, George – who was leading the group – stopped, peering up at two hills in front of them. "Are we on the right track?" he asked his mum uncertainly. "I don't recog-nise this at all... maybe we've gone the wrong way."

Jean looked in the same direction, frowning. "There was only one sand hill near our house, not two... this can't be it."

"We've been going the wrong way this whole time?" whined Lucy, who was getting more and more frustrated with every passing minute.

George thought for a moment. "It's OK, we're probably not that far off course. Let's just go more to the right."

So, they changed their direction and carried on walking, but still they didn't reach their house. After a few hours they were all absolutely exhausted, and when they came across another two sand hills next to each other, Jean said, "I think our house must be nearby."

Mary glanced around. "I don't see any houses here."

"I think we're lost," Lucy replied, sounding angry. "And no surprise really with George guiding us!"

George glared at his sister before suggesting, "Maybe one of those hills *is* our house, just covered in sand?"

"Can you go up and investigate?" his mother asked.

"Sure," he replied, and moments later he was climbing the hill while the rest of his family sat in the shadow it cast on the ground, watching George go and hoping he was going to find something. The heat was unbearable, and by the time he got to the top of the hill, George's whole body was dripping with sweat. He thought longingly of bathing in the spring the day before, then tried to focus on the task at hand.

He turned in a full circle, looking out for any sign of their house, but he couldn't see it anywhere. Perhaps it *was* buried under the sand he was standing on now. Not knowing what else to do, he bent down and started digging into the sand with his bare hands, but every time he tried to dig a hole, more sand would just fall back into it, filling it up again. George carried on digging for several minutes, getting more and more frustrated – not to mention exhausted – but the sand just kept beating him.

"Mum," Lucy said at the bottom of the hill, "I don't think our house is buried under there. This area just isn't familiar to me at all."

Jean was getting more and more annoyed with the situation too, and she snapped at Lucy in response, "Your brother is trying very hard to save us, and you're not helping!"

Mary sighed. "I just hope someone finds us soon and gets us out of this hell!"

Lucy looked up at her brother on the top of the hill, deciding that she'd do a much better job than him. "I'm going up," she told her mother, who warned her to be careful as she started heading up the mound of sand. When she reached George and saw the bad luck he was having trying to dig into the sand, she said, "I don't think the house is under here. We should go and look somewhere else."

Angry now, George stood up and started shouting at his sister. "Well if you know where it is, go and find it, will you? Just leave me alone!"

Lucy rolled her eyes. "Don't be such a drama queen!"

"Drama queen?" he repeated, staring down at his sister. "Do you understand what's happening here? If we don't find the house soon, we're all going to die! Do you understand? Is that getting through your thick brain, Lucy?" Tears were forming in his eyes now, tears of frustration and of pure panic.

Lucy was completely taken aback by her brother's reaction – usually he didn't show any emotion at all – and without saying a word, she kneeled down and continued digging into the sand where George had been digging earlier. There were tears in her eyes too.

After a while, Jean joined them at the top of the hill, helping her two kids dig even deeper into the sand.

Even with their layers of clothes and the hats they wore to protect them from the sun, the heat soon became unbearable, and Jean suggested they stop for a while. "Let's go down to the bottom of the hill and rest for a bit."

Once at the bottom, all four of them had some much-needed water before laying out their blankets in the shadow of the hill. They rested, each of them avoiding looking at the others for fear of seeing the same disappointment they felt reflected back at them. They knew that after the sandstorm, they had very little chance of finding their house; they just didn't want to admit it out loud.

Once they'd rested for a while and had more to drink, Jean lined up the empty bottles in the sand. "We're completely out of water – we'll have to head back to the spring again." Everyone moaned at this, but Jean ignored them. "Come on, we'd better move while we still have some energy left, otherwise we might not make it." Rather reluctantly everyone agreed, and they started walking in what they thought was the direction they'd come from; it was hard to tell for sure.

They'd been going for a mile or so when George saw something in the distance, something that at first he thought must be a mirage. But, as they got closer, the thing became more and more clear: it was smoke. "Look!" shouted George, making everyone jump, "there's smoke coming from somewhere!"

Excitement rippled through the family members and they picked up their pace, wanting to see if it was really true. As they got closer and closer to the smoke, they saw it was coming from a small hut made of clay, and barely believing their eyes, they rushed towards it, almost falling over in their desire to get there.

"There's such a nice smell coming from that hut!" Mary exclaimed. "I wonder what they're cooking!"

"I'm so hungry I could eat anything," Lucy said, licking her lips.

Jean, however, was being a little more reserved. "This is too good to be true…"

As they reached the hut George went over to the entrance-way, which was just a long, ancient curtain – there was no door. "Hello?" he shouted, "Is there anybody here?"

He peered behind the curtain and even though it was dark, he could just about see the interior of the hut, which seemed to be just the one round room. There was a woman at the other end of the room, bent over some kind of stove, and when she heard George's voice, she rushed over. She was old, dressed shabbily, and gave the overall impression of looking a bit like a witch.

She glanced at George and said a few words, but she wasn't speaking English and George could only guess from her tone that she was inviting him in. He looked at the rest of the family, who were standing a few feet away, and shrugged. The old woman beckoned them inside with a hand gesture, and as they entered the little hut, Jean told everyone to be careful.

"It's so dark in here, I can hardly see anything!" Lucy whispered, as they strained their eyes to take in their surroundings. There were no windows and no lamps; the only light was coming from the warm orange glow of the fire the woman was cooking on, although it seemed that it was about to go out. "Wait a minute, I'll be right back," she added, before running out of the hut and over to the sledge to retrieve the torch they'd brought with them. When she got back, she switched on the torch and aimed it at the old woman.

The witch, as Lucy thought of her, had obviously never seen a torch before, and staring at the family in front of her, she started screeching at the top of her lungs. She grabbed a knife and held it over her head, her ugly, warty face now visible in the beam of the torch.

Jean screamed, "Let's go! Run!" and the next moment they were all scrambling to get through the curtain and out into the daylight again. "God knows what that woman was cooking!" Jean gasped as they ran over to the sledge before running off away from the hut. "I was worried she might be a dangerous person!"

Lucy nodded. "She was horrible-looking. Her face was terrifying."

Her mother laughed, though it sounded a little hysterical. "Usually I'd tell you not to judge a book by its cover, but in this case, I think you're right."

As they walked, Mary said, "We could have at least asked her for some take-away. I'm starving."

"No way i was going to eat whatever was on that stove!" Jean replied, and her children agreed.

Making sure the witch woman wasn't following them, they carried on their way, and soon they got to a few more sand hills. By this point everyone was absolutely exhausted, so exhausted in fact that they didn't have the energy or the patience to even try talking to each other much.

"I'm tired," Mary gasped, "I need to have a rest."

Jean nodded. "OK, Mum. Let's all take a break in the shadow behind these hills."

After laying out the blankets they sat down to rest, but soon Lucy got up again. She wanted to be doing something, to keep busy, and she started looking around for any signs of civilisation (other than the witch's house, of course).

As Mary watched her granddaughter she said to Jean, "You know what? I think the house is much more clever than us. As soon as it found out that this place was so hot and the climate was so bad, it just packed up and vanished!" They laughed together at that, glad they could at least find some sort of humour in such a terrible situation.

Just then, Lucy – who was still wandering around – saw something in the sand, and bending down, she realised it was a string. She picked it up and followed it along the ground, eventually finding the balloon it was attached to buried in the sand. Gasping in surprise, she closed her eyes for a minute to try and remember where she'd tied the balloons in relation to the house, and after running in what she hoped was the right direction, she saw four sand hills. The house must be buried under one of them, she thought, and picking one at random she climbed it as fast as she could possibly go.

"I've found it, I've found it!" she yelled happily, dancing up and down. The front of the house was completely covered in sand, so from where they'd been sitting, they never would have even guessed that it was there. But from where Lucy was now standing on the top of the hill, she could just about make out the back of the building. It was the most wonderful sight she'd ever seen.

"I think the heat's got to her," Mary said, laughing. "She must be seeing a mirage."

Jean nodded. "Her brain's probably clogged up with sand – mine certainly feels like it is." Turning to face her daughter, she cupper her hands around her mouth and shouted, "What are you doing, Lucy? There's nothing there, come back!"

When Lucy didn't reply, Jean rolled her eyes. "George, for God's sake go and see what your sister's doing. I think she might be ill."

George did as he was asked, climbing to the top of the hill to reach his sister, but Lucy was also climbing further up the hill, getting further and further away from him. "Come back, Lucy!" he called. "It's just a mirage, there's nothing there!"

Ignoring her brother as usual, Lucy carried on climbing, and once she'd gone behind the hill, she had a much better view of the half of the house that wasn't covered in sand. When George joined her, she pointed at the back of the house. "See, it *is* there – I'm not imagining it."

George gawped, unable to believe his eyes. "It's our house," he whispered in awe, "you were right! It's our house!" They both jumped for joy, George bringing his sister in for a big cuddle as he thanked her. "You did a good job, sis," he said, making her beam with pride.

After having another look at the house to make sure they definitely weren't hallucinating, George and Lucy ran back down the hill and over to their mother and grandmother. "She's telling the truth," George said excitedly, "that's our house, the front is just hidden by the sand!"

Mary gasped as Jean leaped to her feet, hugging and kissing her children as she laughed with delight. "Thank you!" she said. "Thank you for saving my life again! I don't know what I'd do without the two of you."

Lucy smiled, but inside she was welling up. This was the first time in her entire life that she'd actually felt like her whole family loved her. Her mum, her grandma… even George. It was a lovely warming feeling, and she never wanted it to go away.

"Come on," said George, "we should be able to get in the back way," and with that he led his family up and over the sand hill. They all smiled happily as they let themselves in the back door, and even though the house was dark inside (with the sand covering most of the windows), they'd never felt so glad to be back at home.

They took turns washing their hands and faces in a bucket of water before sitting down to drink some water and nibble on some crackers Lucy had found in the back of one of the cupboards. It wasn't the best meal in the world, but everyone was still so relieved to be home that no one really cared that much.

8

AFTER DINNER THEY RETIRED TO BED, SO EXHAUSTED that every single one of them fell asleep straight away, and when they woke up the next morning, it was as if another miracle had occurred in the middle of the night: a strong wind had blown against the house, but this time it had come from the opposite direction and most of the sand that had been covering the building had now vanished.

Jean got up early, and was therefore the first to realise that the sand had gone. She was so happy that it was now light in the house, and she went and woke everybody up straight away, telling them the good news before explaining that they needed to spend the day cleaning the house from top to bottom, and inside to out. First, however, they'd have breakfast.

The day went surprisingly quickly, and by the evening everything was more or less back to normal – apart from, of course, the fact that they were still stranded in a desert. It was the next day that things started to get a little interesting, and it all started while Jean was looking out of her bedroom window.

At first she wasn't sure she was actually seeing what she was seeing, but sure enough, a camel was walking through the desert towards the house, on top of which rode two people. Her first instinct was to jump for joy – they were saved! – but then she thought of the witch in the cottage, and decided that perhaps these people weren't here to save them at all.

Running downstairs, Jean told everyone of what she'd seen and then ordered them to lock all the doors and windows. "They might be here to rob us," she said, her voice shaking with panic.

George wasted no time in running and getting his gun from the cabinet, and after what had happened last time with the wild dogs, he made sure to prepare his bullets properly.

Lucy was getting a little scared. "Are they armed, Mum?"

"I don't know."

"They might be here to help us," suggested Mary. "Oh, do let them come in; we could use the company, couldn't we? And anyway, they might be able to tell us where we are."

"I don't know," repeated Jean, frowning, "they might be criminals."

"And they might not," Mary pointed out.

Just then George came running in, having been watching the approaching guests from his bedroom window. "It's a girl about my age and a man who looks like he could be her father," he explained. "He's almost falling off the camel – he looks sick."

"See," said Mary, "you don't have to leap to conclusions about everyone being criminals all the time."

Jean sighed. "OK, fine. If they need help, we'll see what we can do."

George opened the front door just as the girl was jumping down from the camel. She then helped her father down before tying the rope that was around the animal's neck to a small pole that she slammed into the ground.

George ran out to talk to her. "Hi, my name's George and I live here with my family. Do you need help? Is that your dad?"

The girl stared at him in confusion – as though she hadn't understood a word he'd said – and when she replied, she did so in the strange, ancient-sounding language that the witch woman had used in the cottage.

Shaking his head, George gestured at her father. "Come, let's get him inside."

She seemed to understand the gist of what George was saying, and she let him support her father into the house, where she nodded at Jean, Mary, and Lucy as if in greeting. George helped her father over to the sofa in the lounge before lowering him down onto the comfortable seat. The girl sat beside him.

Wanting to help now that she'd realised they weren't criminals, Jean brought over a couple of bottles of water that they'd filled from the pit outside, as well as some leftover crackers and biscuits. She handed them to the girl, who smiled back gratefully.

They all watched as the girl gave some water to her father, then drank some herself before tucking into the food. She glanced around the lounge while she ate, whereas her father just closed his eyes as he relaxed back into the sofa.

It was utterly silent in the room, and as Mary was getting a little uncomfortable she decided to ask the girl, "Where do you come from? Do you know where we are? What country? We're a little lost, you see," she explained.

The girl responded in the same strange language as before, which sounded as if it were at least a thousand years old.

Mary shrugged. "Anyone have any ideas what she said?"

Jean shook her head. "Perhaps she's speaking Arabic? I don't know… we could try some kind of sign language?"

Before anyone got a chance to answer, the man on the sofa grabbed the girl's hand, whispering something in her ear as tears filled his eyes. The girl said something back, her tone one of complete distress, and when her father collapsed against the back of the sofa and slowly closed his eyes, she started wailing uncontrollably.

"Oh God," said Jean, "he didn't just… *die*… did he?"

The girl was leaning over her father, pressing her fingers onto his neck as if to try and find a pulse. Her expression told them everything they needed to know.

Every member of the family had tears in their eyes as they watched the awful scene unfold in front of them, and Mary was shaking her head rather violently. "Oh no, this is terrible!" she exclaimed. "Has he really just passed away?"

"I think so," said George quietly, who was watching the man very closely. He wasn't moving. He wasn't breathing. He was gone.

Slowly, so as not to startle her, Jean went and sat next to the girl, patting her on the back to try and comfort her. The girl responded by flinging herself into Jean's arms, gasping out words as she cried into Jean's shoulder. Of course, the family couldn't understand any of them.

"What are we going to do?" asked Mary.

"We have to help them," Jean said as she pulled back from the hug and smiled at the girl. "We have to bury her father's body."

There was silence in the room for a moment, and then, quietly, George stood up and left the lounge, heading to the garage where he retrieved a shovel. Outside, he started digging a grave for the girl's father, although that was easier said than done in the sand. He stopped briefly to fetch a bucket of water for the camel, who started drinking greedily, and then he carried on, digging and digging as deep as he could go.

When he was finished, he headed back inside to announce that the grave was ready.

Jean brought him in for a hug. "Thank you for doing that, George. We've tried to communicate to the girl what we're going to do, and I think she understands."

"George?" the girl asked, in her strange accent.

It was the first word she'd said that they could actually understand, and George smiled eagerly, pointing to himself as he repeated, "George." He looked at his family, pointing at them one by one as he said their names. "Jean. Mary. Lucy." Then, rather tentatively, he pointed his finger at the girl, raising his eyebrows.

After a moment, the girl pointed at herself and said, "Laila."

Everyone in the room smiled, and Jean said, "Welcome to our home, Laila. It's nice to meet you."

After a brief silence, Jean walked over to Laila and pointed at her father before pointing at the door. "It's time to take him outside. OK?"

More or less getting the gist of what Jean was saying, Laila nodded sadly, and together with Jean and George, they lifted

the body of her father and carried him outside before lowering him gently into the grave.

Mary, and Lucy watched as Jean, Laila and George covered
the body in sand, and when they were finished, Laila took a
small piece of engraved leather from her pocket and dropped
it on the top, whispering a few words in her language at the
same time.

After everyone had stood there in respectful silence for a
minute or two, Jean took Laila's hand and walked her back
inside while George took the camel and led it into the garage
for safety; he didn't want any wild animals attacking it, or for
it to get lost in a heap of sand if another storm hit.

That night, Laila sat with them at the dining table for
dinner, and after a bit of discussion, Mary offered to share
her room with the girl. She was clearly so exhausted, and she
happily let herself be led upstairs to Mary's bed. As soon as
she lay down, she was out like a light.

9

THE NEXT MORNING, GEORGE KNOCKED ON HIS GRAND-
mother's door and Mary called out, "Come in, I'm awake!"

When George opened the door, he saw that Laila was still
lying in the bed while Mary sat in a chair nearby. "How's she
doing?" he asked his grandmother.

"She's OK I think," Mary replied, "but after sleeping for
an hour or two she woke up and started crying. I tried to
comfort her but it didn't work, and I didn't get much sleep
either." She peered up at her grandson. "Maybe you can
help her?"

George shrugged. "I wish I could, but you know I don't
understand her language."

"Well, in that case, your mission is to teach her *our* language and *our* customs. Do you think you can do that?"

George had no idea if he could do that, but he supposed
he should at least give it a try; it must be so hard for Laila,

he thought, not only to lose her father but to be surrounded by strangers she couldn't understand. Walking over to her, he said rather timidly, "Hello, how are you today?"

Laila quickly sat up, climbing out of the bed as she mumbled something in her language, causing George to turn to his grandmother and shrug. "I have no idea what she said."

Lucy – who had clearly been listening from the corridor – suddenly appeared in the doorway. "George, she wants you to go away and leave her alone." She sighed, shaking her head. "You boys just don't understand these things."

Suddenly embarrassed, George's cheeks turned red as he said, "She could be right. I'd better go."

When he'd left, Mary smiled at Lucy. "Why don't you take Laila downstairs and show her where to wash her hands and face? I'm sure it'll be time for breakfast soon."

Mary was right, and within a few minutes everyone had gathered in the kitchen and were sitting at the table, ready to eat. Laila was staring at the cutlery as if she'd never seen anything like it in her life – the night before they'd just had sandwiches and had used their hands – and she watched people eat the cereal with their spoons with something akin to wonder on her face. She soon learned how to use her own spoon, and as she ate she asked questions that nobody could answer; it was all a little awkward and confusing.

"I wish we could communicate with her," Jean said sadly, and everyone agreed. Laila just smiled and carried on eating.

After breakfast, Lucy took Laila up to her room, where they sat on her bed as Lucy showed Laila her photo album, which featured hundreds of photos of her family and friends in America. While Laila looked through the pictures, seemingly finding each one more fascinating than the last, Lucy put some music on her iPod. Laila stared at the little device in awe – she was just so wonderstruck at everything in this new and different world.

After a while, Lucy started pointing at different objects in her room, saying the name for the object out loud and then getting Laila to repeat it. Laila looked confused at first, but once she realised what Lucy was doing, she became much more enthusiastic – it was like they were playing a game, and Laila wanted to show her new friend that she was good at it.

Lucy had just shown Laila her old teddy bear that she kept on the top of her wardrobe when Laila leaped up from the bed, pointing out the window and drawing some imaginary humps in the air. Realising that she was asking about her camel, Lucy took Laila's hand and led her out of her bedroom and into George's. "She wants to see her camel," she told him. "Is it in the garage?"

"Yes," George replied, smiling shyly at Laila. "Come on, I'll take you to him."

Once they'd got to the garage and had let the camel outside, George wandered off into the desert for a few hours, coming back with some desert bushes for it to eat. He then filled the bucket with water again and placed it in front of the camel. Laila smiled at him in response, as if to thank him for his help, and all of George's earlier embarrassment vanished completely.

For the rest of the day, Laila, Lucy, and George spent time with the camel, which to the brother and sister was something new and interesting to look at; after all, they had no TV or radio to entertain themselves with.

First of all the siblings started petting the camel, and once it had got used to them, Lucy turned to Laila and mimed riding it. Understanding what she meant, Laila pulled on the rope around the camel's neck and when it sat down on the sand, she helped Lucy climb on top of the large animal. Lucy was a little scared, but Laila comforted her with sign language and a pat on the shoulder before climbing on next to Lucy. She said something in her language and the camel responded, standing up slowly – if it had moved any faster, Lucy would have fallen off, and she held on for dear life as it got to its feet.

George watched as the camel started walking, laughing at the sight of his small sister on such a huge animal, and when they got back from their ride, it was George's turn to get on. It felt a little strange sitting between the humps, but it also felt good to be travelling through the desert without having to walk everywhere.

Jean and Mary watched from the front door, smiling. "This camel is really useful," Jean commented, "we can use it to carry our stuff – and us."

Mary nodded in agreement, laughing when Lucy ran over to them and exclaimed, "Can we keep the camel? I want to call him Cammie!"

Jean laughed too. "I think that can be arranged," she replied, smiling widely. Things certainly seemed to be looking up.

Over the next few days all of the family got to know Laila better, and despite the language barrier, their communication improved with every passing day. George and Lucy also improved at riding the camel, and one day George suggested that he take Laila hunting with him. After some sign language and miming involving shooting, animals, and eating, Laila understood what he was saying, and nodded in agreement. George said the word, "Hunting," and Laila replied, "Hunting, yes."

"I want to go too!" Lucy exclaimed, aiming the words at her mum rather than at George.

"That's fine with me," Jean replied, and George – who had been looking forward to spending some time alone with Laila – mumbled rather reluctantly, "OK, whatever."

Heading upstairs, George and Lucy changed their clothes, finding some of their mum's casual clothing to give to Laila before gathering up all the equipment they'd need and placing it in a heap next to the camel. George – who had been practising giving commands to the camel – repeated the word Laila had taught him, and the camel sat down on the sand so they could load him up with their belongings. Lucy and Laila sat on the camel's back as they headed off into the desert, while George walked beside them, the shotgun in his hand.

When they got to the oasis, Laila ordered the camel to sit down so she could jump off, and when she tried to help Lucy get down, she insisted on getting off by herself, which she just about managed to do without stumbling and falling over.

They walked over to the spring, enjoying the fresh water as they washed their hands and faces; Laila cheered up considerably after she'd had a wash, beaming at George and Lucy as though the spring were the best thing in the world. The camel drank while they filled up several water bottles, and then they rested under some nearby palms, eating dates from the trees while they listened to music from Lucy's iPod. She had to be careful about how often she used it – as they didn't have any electricity to charge it up once it had run out of power – but seeing how much their new guest seemed to love music, Lucy couldn't help but get it out and put on some of her favourite songs. George seemed to be having fun too, singing along to the tracks and miming out some of the words to Laila, who found the whole thing extremely amusing.

After a while Laila stood up and headed over to the spring again, where she jumped in and started swimming. George joined her, and soon they were splashing each other with water and screaming with laughter. Lucy watched them from under the palm trees, feeling a little left out and more than a little jealous, but she didn't say anything.

As they got out of the water and walked over to the palm trees, Lucy noticed they were holding hands, and after lying down again under the tree, they started talking to each other, sometimes using English words, other times using their own special form of sign language. They laughed at their communication problems, and again when Laila tried to sing along to songs with no idea what the words were.

Lucy watched on, her feelings of jealousy and resentment almost boiling over. She felt like she shouldn't be there – that she was intruding on a special moment – and after a couple more minutes, she stood up and announced she was going on a walk.

George was so preoccupied with talking to Laila that he didn't notice how sad or annoyed his little sister seemed to be, and he waved her away as he replied rather absentmindedly, "OK, but don't go too far."

"Don't miss me too much!" Lucy moaned before walking off, and once she was gone, George turned back to face Laila.

She was so beautiful, he thought, and her smile was amazing – if only he could communicate that to her! Instead, he looked at her in a loving way and said, slowly, "I like you very much and I hope you feel the same way."

Clearly not understanding what he was saying, Laila just repeated the words back to him: "I like you very much and I hope you feel the same way."

George smiled. For now, it would do.

10

MEANWHILE, LUCY WAS LISTENING TO HER IPOD AS SHE strolled near a hill, and was just peering inside a hole in the stone wall she'd found when she heard a horrifying noise coming from behind her.

Turning around, she was terrified to see a huge lion sitting on the hilltop, staring down at her, his eyes fixated on hers. She'd never seen any animal look so powerful or strong before, and even though for a second she was frozen to the spot, she just about managed to leap into the hole in the wall – dropping her iPod outside in the process – before the lion ran over to her.

Lucy's heart was pumping madly in her chest, and she was absolutely convinced she was about to be eaten, but when she looked up at the entrance of the hole, she realised it was too small for the lion to fit his body through. He swiped one of his large, furry paws into the hole, trying to grab her, but it was no good.

She sighed in relief; she was safe… for now. "Better luck next time," she mumbled under her breath, though her voice shook as she said it.

After a while – and a few more swipes of his paw – the lion walked away from the hole, though he sat nearby as if guarding his prey. Lucy groaned; what with George being so preoccupied with his new girlfriend, she could be stuck in here forever!

"God help me," she whispered to herself as a tear slid down her cheek.

Back under the palm trees, Laila looked around, frowning. "Lucy?" she asked.

George understood what she meant, and realising that his sister hadn't come back from her walk, he started to grow concerned. It had been at least a couple of hours since she'd left. "Where is she? Come on, let's go and look." He stood up and held his hand out to Laila, pulling her to her feet, and soon they were walking in the direction Lucy had gone. He took his shotgun with him just in case.

Meanwhile, in the hole, Lucy was growing more and more frightened with every passing minute. What if the lion never moved? She would starve to death, or perhaps die of thirst, here in this dank, dark hole. Neither option seemed good.

It had been a while since she'd either seen or heard the lion, however, so crawling over to the entrance of the hole, she peered out. Instantly, the lion – who had clearly been waiting just out of sight for her to do exactly that – pounced, his claws just about touching Lucy on the hand as she scrambled away from the entrance.

She looked down at her palm, which was scratched and bleeding, and started to cry. "Please leave me alone!" she wailed, all feelings of hope draining out of her. "Please!"

The lion roared in response, and a few metres away, George and Laila heard the terrifying sound, stopping in their tracks. George immediately started running in the direction of the roar, and when he saw the lion lying down beside the hole, he turned and yelled at Laila, "Get away from here! This animal is very dangerous!"

Ignoring him, Laila pointed at the sand, where Lucy's footprints could be seen leading into the hole. Nodding, George held the shotgun in front of him and took a few steps forward. He could see Lucy's iPod lying on the ground and a shockwave of fear ran through his entire body. If that lion had harmed her in any way…

He shook his head, trying to focus, and just as the lion looked up at him, he pressed the trigger. He shot just to the right of the large animal in the hopes of scaring him away, and it worked – the lion leaped up and ran off.

Making sure the lion had definitely gone, George glanced at Laila before running over to the hole. "Lucy?" he yelled. "Are you in there?"

"George!" came Lucy's voice – shaking and scared – from inside the hole, and as she scrambled over to the entrance she added, "Where have you been? Do you know how long I've been hiding in here?" She started crying uncontrollably. "I thought I was going to die! How could you?"

"I'm sorry," George replied, hanging his head down. He didn't know what else he could say; he felt terrible.

Smiling at Lucy, Laila took her scratched hand and poured some water over it from the bottle she'd been carrying, and after washing the wound, she wrapped a piece of cloth around it. Lucy nodded in response; she couldn't quite bring herself to say thank you.

"Right," said George, looking around to check the coast was clear. "Let's go home, shall we?"

When they got back home, Lucy ran up to her mother and hugged her tightly. When Jean asked what on earth was the matter, Lucy told her everything while George hovered in the background, his cheeks glowing red with embarrassment and shame.

"OK Lucy," Jean said eventually. "Why don't you climb into bed and get some rest? You'll feel better afterwards."

Lucy ran upstairs without even looking at her brother or Laila, and when she was gone, Jean turned to her son. "I trusted you to look after her, George."

He hung his head. "I know. I'm sorry. It won't happen again."

Jean sighed. "It better not."

Up in her room, before getting into bed, Lucy looked out of her window, her cheeks still stained with tears. "God," she said, "please can you make some lightning tonight? I don't want to be stuck here any longer – especially not with George and Laila here too."

Nothing happened – not that she really expected it to – and sighing, she got into bed and snuggled down under the covers.

11

DAYS TURNED INTO WEEKS, WEEKS TURNED INTO MONTHS, and soon the family had come to accept that they'd likely never see America ever again. It was a difficult and horrible idea to get used to, but they were slowly settling into their lives in the desert, trying to make the best of things and keeping their spirits high.

George was probably the only member of the family who wasn't missing home at all – he had fallen head over heels for Laila, and he spent most of his days teaching her English, a great excuse for hanging out with her all day. Being surrounded by solely English speakers had done wonders for her development, and she was now almost fluent. She'd even been learning to read, borrowing Lucy's books and asking George whenever she came across words she didn't understand.

Yes, George was pretty happy with how things were going, even if the rest of his family weren't.

One day, George and Laila headed back out into the desert (Lucy had absolutely refused to go anywhere with them ever again), riding the camel to the oasis and laughing and joking the whole way.

The aim of this particular trip was to hunt a deer for dinner, and after hitting one in the neck on his first try, George lay the body of the animal next to the camel before getting in the spring with Laila. With no Lucy looking on disapprovingly, they were free to do as they liked – dunking their heads underwater, splashing each other, and having swimming races.

Once they'd tired themselves out, they got out of the water and lay down under the palm trees. Laila looked so pretty that George couldn't resist hugging her, and as they pulled apart from each other, he kissed her on the lips. "I love you," he whispered, looking at her intently, and she smiled and said the words back to him. This time, she knew exactly what she was saying.

* * *

Back at the house, Lucy was just fetching some water from the pit when she heard a strange sound behind her, and turning to look, she saw the hyena. It was staring at her, growling, and Lucy had a rather horrific flashback to the lion prowling after her while she'd been stuck in that hole.

"No!" she shouted out, trying to appear braver than she actually felt, "Not this time!" Then, running into the house, she slammed the door behind her before rushing over to the gun cabinet.

"What's happened?" Jean asked, having heard her daughter yelling.

"It's that hyena!" Lucy shouted back as she took out her father's pistol. "I'm going to do what George should have done before – I'm going to kill him!"

After running back to the front door, Lucy kicked it open before opening fire on the hyena, shooting it in the leg and injuring it badly. The animal howled in pain but limped off before Lucy could get another shot at it, and as it retreated she shouted out, "I warned you, didn't I?!"

Walking over to Lucy, Jean quickly grabbed the pistol off her. "You shouldn't be using that at your age!" she said, surprised at how her daughter had acted.

Lucy shrugged. "We're not in America anymore. I don't think the usual rules apply."

Jean didn't answer – after all, her daughter was probably right.

* * *

Back at the oasis, George and Laila were still sitting under the palm trees, holding each other's hands as they talked.

Laila looked sad, and when George asked what was wrong, she just said the words, "I have a problem."

"What is it?" George asked. "Maybe I can help."

Laila sighed, taking a moment to try and think of the right words to explain. "I have more family. Sisters, a brother... I have to get them. To find them."

"Find them?"

"Yes, they think I... I am lost. And I don't know where they are."

George nodded. "Don't worry; we'll help you. Come on, let's get home and we can talk more about it there."

Laila nodded, but when George stood up to get the camel, it broke free of its rope and ran off before he even knew what was happening.

Laila shouted something in her language and George ran off after the camel, following it for several hundred metres before it halted and he was able to catch up with it. Grabbing what was left of the rope, George got the camel under control and started heading back to Laila, but when he got to the palm trees, there was no sight of her. He could just about hear her voice in the distance, calling his name, but then it was gone.

Panic filled every inch of his body. Had Laila been taken? And if so, by whom? How would he ever get her back? How would he even know where to start?

Not knowing what else to do, George quickly loaded the deer onto the camel and then, shaking with fear and worry, he rushed back home, where he found his mother and explained what had happened. By the end of it, he was crying freely.

"It's OK, son," she said, trying to comfort him while Mary patted him on the arm. "We'll figure it out."

"I need to go and find her," George said. "I can't live without her!"

Jean looked horrified at the thought. "And *I* can't live without *you*! What if you get captured too?"

"I'll be careful," he replied. "I *have* to do this."

Jean was crying now, holding onto her son tightly, and when George promised he'd come back, Lucy appeared at his side and said, "Let him go, Mum. I can look after you until he gets home again."

Jean smiled at her daughter, then reluctantly let George start preparing for his trip.

He took as many guns and bullets as he could carry, packed some food and water and some equipment he might need, and after saying goodbye to his family, he headed out on the camel, disappearing into the darkness.

The light from the moon lit his way, and when he got to the oasis, he turned on the torch he'd brought with him and started searching for clues. He soon found some camel's footprints that didn't belong to the one he was currently riding, and after taking a deep breath, he started following them into the desert.

A few hours later, the sun was just starting to rise when George came to a few huts that appeared to be made from mud and clay. After tying his camel to a tree, he slowly walked over to the nearest hut, being as quiet as possible as he climbed the exterior clay wall and peeked over. There were several men there, resting, and he immediately knew that these were the kidnappers who had taken Laila – he just had a feeling, deep down in his gut.

Climbing back down the wall, he made his way over to the next hut, climbing up again and peering over to see a few prisoners sitting on the ground, tied up with rope. Laila was with them, and when he saw her, his heart soared.

There were a couple of guards next to the prisoners, but they were sleeping too, so after climbing down on the other side of the wall, George made his way carefully over to Laila. The other prisoners watched him as he went, but thankfully they didn't say anything.

When Laila saw him, she opened her mouth wide, then shook her head as he crouched down next to her. "These people are dangerous," she whispered. "Be careful!"

George smiled at her, whispering back, "Don't worry about me," as he took out his pocketknife and started cutting the rope from her wrists and ankles.

When she was free, she hugged him tightly before taking the knife off him. "We need to help the others," she explained, and George kept his eyes on the guards as she freed the other prisoners. It was only then that George realised some of the prisoners were children, and as she cut them free, a couple of them started crying loudly.

Alarmed, George glanced back at the guards, but it was too late – the children's cries had woken them up.

By now Laila was helping the women and the children climb over the wall to freedom, but seconds later the guards rushed over and started hitting them, slapping them to the ground. Getting more and more angry at what he was witnessing, George decided to start shooting the guards, and upon hearing the sound of the shots fired, the men from the other hut ran over. As they appeared at the top of the wall, George shot at them too, causing some to fall down while others just ran away.

A few of the prisoners – who had never seen a gun before, let alone what one could do to a human body – fell to the ground then, worshipping George as if he were a god. Even under the terrible circumstances, George couldn't believe what he is witnessing,

"Quick, we need to go!" shouted Laila, and George nodded.

After everyone had been helped over the wall, and after George had checked there were no other guards or kidnappers around, he left the women and children what little food and water he'd brought with him before getting back on the camel with Laila.

She said something to the other prisoners in her language, and then they set off, heading back into the desert. As they went, Laila clung onto George tightly.

He couldn't believe he'd saved her, and thinking back to how the prisoners had reacted to him wielding the gun, he smiled. Right now, he *felt* like a god!

That night, when George and Laila got back home, the rest of the family were so pleased that they had a big party to celebrate, with singing and dancing and a *lot* of laughing.

Everyone was just so happy to have Laila back, but none more so than George, who went to sleep that night with wonderful images of Laila dancing through his mind.

He could rest again. She was safe.

* * *

A few days later, things had got – more or less – back to normal in the house, and Lucy was getting restless; she was bored of being cooped up all day, so she jumped at the chance to go to the oasis with George and Laila to collect wood and desert bushes for the fire.

It was while they were doing so that they heard the sound of hooves coming towards them, and while George's first thought was that it might be the kidnappers again, it soon became apparent that it was something else entirely: approaching from the distance there were about twenty horses, as well as a ornate chariot – obviously containing someone very important indeed. It didn't, however, look at all modern.

In fact, it looked like something Lucy had once seen in one of her books on Ancient Egypt.

The minute Laila saw the chariot she bowed her head, whispering, "It's the Prince of Egypt!" to George and Lucy as it approached.

George bowed his head too, but Lucy was having none of it. "I don't care who he is!" she shouted defiantly. "I'm not going to bow for a stranger!"

The chariot passed by without stopping, going over the hill and disappearing from view, and George was just about to ask Laila how she knew it was the prince when they heard a series of horrible crashes and shouts coming from the direction in which the chariot had just gone.

Rushing over to the top of the hill to see what was happening, George's jaw dropped when he took in the view before them: a group of rebels had attacked the chariot, and were now taking part in hand-to-hand combat with what must have been the prince's royal guards.

George thought about heading down there with his gun but then decided against it; he'd be severely outnumbered and he didn't want to leave the girls on their own.

He was just wondering what he could do to help when a man ran up the hill towards the three of them. Going by his well-made clothes, this was the prince, and he was gasping and sweating as he reached them; he looked like he was about to collapse.

He was just making his way over to Laila when George noticed three rebels in the distance, scrambling up the hill after the prince, and bringing up his shotgun, George fired at the rebels, shooting them dead. The prince stared at George in amazement, then started asking what sounded like several questions in his native language.

Laila took the prince's arm, speaking to him in the same language, and as she spoke, understanding filtered through into his features.

When Laila was finished, she turned to face George and Lucy. "This is Prince Kinan, an old friend."

"You know each other?" George asked, surprised.

Laila nodded. "Yes, for a long time. He says he wants to thank you for saving his life." She gestured at the shotgun.

Lucy, who had been studying the prince intently, said, "You're hurt. Your arm is bleeding. You can come with us – we have a house and we can make you better."

Laila translated, everyone agreed, and soon they were back home, introducing the prince to Jean and Mary. They were both ecstatic to have a guest in the house, and even more so when they realised that their guest was royalty.

After thanking everyone for their hospitality – through Laila – the prince wandered around the house, looking at everything intently while the others watched.

"I can't believe we have a prince here!" Jean exclaimed. "So we're in Egypt, then! Do you think he can help us get back to America?"

Lucy sighed. "He can barely help himself, let alone do anything for us."

George nodded. 'And, I don't know how… but going by the prince and the chariot he was in – not to mention everything else we've seen – we're in *Ancient* Egypt. Not modern-day Egypt.'

Jean laughed. 'Don't be silly; that's not possible,' but when no one replied, she fell silent. Considering everything that had happened to them, *anything* was possible.

Half an hour later they all sat down for lunch, Prince Kinan and Laila conversing in their language while everyone else listened politely, even though they didn't understand a word of what they were saying. The prince would occasionally try and talk to the family using sign language, but it soon became clear that he was getting tired and needed to rest after the incident with the rebels.

Once they'd finished eating, Jean said to Laila, "Will you take the prince up to George's room? He can have a rest there."

Laila nodded, and George went with them. After putting the prince into bed, he started to leave the room.

"Are you coming?" he asked Laila, but she shook her head.

"I want to stay. Make sure Kinan is alright."

She was staring at the prince, smiling, and something about the way she was looking at Kinan made George feel intensely jealous all of a sudden. He wished he could speak fluent Egyptian; perhaps then he and Laila would be able to get closer.

George left the room, heading back downstairs, and when he sat down at the table and started staring into space, Jean went over to him. "What's the matter?" she asked. "Are you coming down with something?"

Lucy laughed. "The only thing he's coming down with is heartbreak! It's clear the prince and Laila go well together."

George glared at his little sister while Jean shook her head. "Don't pay any attention to her," she said, making Lucy giggle even more. "It's obvious that Laila likes you."

George wasn't so sure, and as he waited and waited for Laila to come downstairs, he started to doubt that she had ever liked him. Why did she need to spend this much time at the prince's bedside?

Finally, hours later, she appeared in the kitchen, smiling.

"How's Kinan? Did you see to his wound?" Jean asked.

"His wound? Yes," Laila replied, before adding, "but he is hungry."

"No problem," said Jean, handing a plate of sandwiches over to Laila. "I made these for him in case he woke up. Would you take them upstairs?" She pointed at the staircase and Laila nodded.

"Thank you," she said, before heading back upstairs. She hadn't even looked at George.

He waited some more, and when Laila came down again – this time with the empty plate – he took her to one side, where no one else would be able to hear them. "Do you still love me?" he asked, almost scared to hear the answer.

Laila smiled. "Yes, I love you. And I thank you for saving me. But… Kinan, he can help. Help find my family."

George nodded sadly. He wanted Laila to find her family, of course he did, but he also knew that would probably mean losing her in the process. "I understand," he said, before walking away.

That night, George slept in Lucy's room while Lucy bunked in with Jean, and the next morning, he was woken by the sound of people talking and laughing: it was Laila and Kinan.

Not wanting to listen to them having fun, George headed downstairs and made breakfast for everyone, something Jean and Mary very much appreciated.

As the family ate (Laila and Kinan had their breakfast in George's room), Lucy asked, "Are we going out today?"

George shook his head. "No, I can't. I'm… not feeling well."

Lucy raised her eyebrows. "You can't go anywhere without her, can you? You don't want to leave her here with *him*."

"Just leave me alone, Lucy!" he snapped. "I'm not in the mood for you."

"Fine," said Lucy, who was beginning to get a bit bored of her brother's moping. "I'm going for a walk outside, around the house."

Jean smiled at her daughter. "Don't go too far. Just around the house, OK?"

"OK," Lucy replied, but as soon as she was out of her mother's view, she headed into the garage instead, untying the camel and riding it off into the desert in the direction of the oasis. She didn't want to sneak around behind her mother's back, but she knew there was no way she'd let her go on her own, and she just *had* to get out of that house. Since Laila and Kinan had arrived, things weren't so fun anymore.

Putting her headphones on, Lucy listened to her iPod as the camel travelled further and further into the desert, and soon her eyelids started to droop. She was so tired she decided to close her eyes, just for a minute…

She woke up with a start, and looking around at their surroundings, she realised she had no idea where they were. How long had she been asleep for? Going by how far the sun had moved in the sky it had been a good few hours, and the camel had clearly changed direction at some point making them very, very lost!

Panic was rising up inside Lucy as she jumped off the camel to look around. She was hoping she would see the camel's footprints in the sand that she'd be able to follow back home, but it was windy and all signs of their tracks had been swept away. "No!" she wailed, glaring at the camel. "Why did you do this? Now we might die out here!"

Just then a snake jumped out from a nearby bush, causing Lucy to jump and the camel to run off, the rope dragging behind it as it went. A piece of the rope fell off and landed in the sand.

Shouting, Lucy picked up the rope and started running after the camel, tears streaming down her face as she tried to keep up. "Please, Cammie!" she yelled. "Don't leave me on my own!"

The camel was getting further and further away, and within seconds it had disappeared from view behind the sand hills. Lucy stopped to catch her breath, shaking her head as she looked at the piece of rope in her hands. "Well, at least he left me something to hang myself with," she muttered, before bursting into tears again.

At least now she could see the camel's footprints, and after wiping her tears away and trying to get herself under control, Lucy followed in its tracks.

She was so focused on looking at the individual footprints, however, that she didn't notice how the actual ground around her was changing and before she even realised what was happening, she found herself getting pulled downwards by a strong yet invisible force.

She'd learned about quicksand at school but she had no idea what you were supposed to do if you got trapped in it, and the more she struggled to get out, the further down it pulled her, until she was buried up to her chest in sand.

After coming to the conclusion that the more she moved, the more she sank, Lucy tried to calm down and stop shifting. This was easier said than done, but she soon managed to get her arms free, and as she still had the piece of rope in her hands, she made it into a hook and threw it out of the quicksand pit. She was hoping against hope that Cammie would come back and somehow put his foot through the loop to drag her out, but she thought that was maybe expecting too much from a camel.

"Cammie!" she cried as sweat ran down her face. "Please help me!" Her mouth was dry and the words came out all croaky, but still she kept on trying. "I'm stuck! Help!"

She desperately wanted to get the attention of the camel, but as it turned out, she ended up getting the attention of something else instead: a hyena. A rather large hyena. And one who looked very, very hungry.

It was staring at her as it approached, but upon realising that Lucy was stuck in the quicksand, it stopped walking towards her and started circling the pit instead.

"Go away!" she cried as more tears streamed down her face. "Leave me alone!" By now she was completely distraught, and absolutely convinced that she was going to die out there in the desert. The only question in her mind was how – would it be the quicksand? The hyena? Or would she simply collapse from thirst and dehydration?

Now incredibly frustrated, Lucy grabbed a fistful of sand and threw it at the hyena, who jumped back and got its paw stuck in the loop of the rope. Instinctively, Lucy pulled on the rope with both hands and the hyena pulled back, dragging Lucy out of the quicksand at the same time.

Hardly able to believe her luck, Lucy grabbed more sand as she was dragged out of the pit, and when she was able to stand again, she flung the sand in the hyena's face, causing it to run off with the rope still tied around its leg.

Without wasting any more time, Lucy carried on following the camel's footprints, and when she saw the shape of the animal a few hundred metres in front of her, her heart leaped in hope. This hope was short-lived, however, when she realised there were two men standing next to it, their own camels watching on as they rifled through Lucy's belongings.

"Hey!" she yelled as she ran towards them. "That's my camel! I need to take him home with me!"

The two men looked up from what they were doing, saw the little girl coming towards them, then went back to rifling through the bags on Cammie's back. One of the men started laughing.

Frustrated, Lucy pulled on the rope around her camel's neck, trying to get it to move, but the men didn't like that at all – one of them slapped her around the face, making her fall down and land on the sand.

Lucy watched, feeling helpless, as they continued looking through her stuff, but when they pulled out the pistol and – clearly not understanding what it was – threw it on the ground, she grabbed it and aimed it at their heads. "Give me back my camel or I'll shoot!" she yelled, knowing they wouldn't be able to understand her but not really caring.

One of the men laughed again, taking a stick out of his belt and hitting Lucy on the shoulder, and in retaliation, she aimed the gun at his leg and fired. He cried out with pain, and as the other man turned and headed towards her, pulling what looked like a knife out of his robes, she shot him in the arm.

Now clearly terrified of the little girl with the magic weapon, the two men leaped onto their camels and rode off into the distance.

"Finally," Lucy said, now more angry than upset, as she climbed onto Cammie's back and held the pistol against the camel's head. "Now," she continued, "let's get some things straight. I nearly drowned in quicksand, because of you. I nearly got eaten by a hyena, because of you. And I nearly got beaten to death by two strangers, because of you. I swear to God, if you take the wrong path home, I'm going to kill you." Then, putting the pistol away, she kicked the camel's side and they started off in what she hoped was the direction of home.

12

BACK AT THE HOUSE, EVERYONE WAS SO PREOCCUPIED with making George feel better that no one had noticed how long Lucy had been gone for. It had now got to the point when even Jean was fed up with George's moping, and so she'd convinced him to go and talk to Laila again.

She was still in his room with Prince Kinan, and not wanting to do this in front of him but knowing he wouldn't be able to understand anyway, George knocked on the door and let himself in.

"Laila," he said, "I'd like to talk to you." He glanced at the prince briefly. "If that's OK?"

Laila smiled. "Of course. What is it?"

"I just want to know what's going on, really," George replied, annoyed with how vague he sounded. He wanted to ask what was going on between the two of them specifically, but even knowing that the prince wouldn't understand, he found that the words just wouldn't come out.

Laila thought for a moment, then sat down on the floor, gesturing for George to do the same. "You should know my story – my family's story," she started. You see, my father was a very important member of the royal family; he had a good relationship with Prince Kinan."

George coughed. "I see. I didn't know that, I'm sorry."

Laila nodded. "My father had many enemies, people who tried to plot against him, who tried to kill him and my whole family. So my father and I ran away, which is when he got injured. Prince Kinan has since told me that my brother and sisters were put in jail, so although they're alive, they're not exactly safe." She paused for a moment, staring into the distance. "The last words my father said to me were, 'Whenever you find an opportunity, you need to save your brother and sisters from prison.' Now, Kinan hopes he can help me. I hope so too."

George hung his head in shame; he was so embarrassed that he'd spent all this time worrying about himself when Laila had far bigger problems to be dealing with. "I'm sorry I've been so selfish. If I can do anything to help, just let me know."

"Thank you," Laila replied. "I know you love me and would do anything for me, but right now, you cannot help."

George nodded sadly, and was just about to respond when he heard his mother shouting from downstairs. She sounded frantic, panicked.

"What's wrong?" he asked as he made his way down the stairs and into the kitchen.

"Have you seen Lucy?" Jean asked, rushing over to her son and placing her hands on his shoulders. "We can't find her! We've looked everywhere!"

Mary was hovering nearby, clearly worried. "She said she was just going for a walk around the house, but that was *hours* ago!"

George thought for a moment, frowning as he thought back to earlier. "Lucy was annoyed that I wouldn't go to the oasis with her – perhaps that's where she is? She may have just lost track of time." Remembering the lion, he hoped against hope that what he'd said was true.

Just then, Laila appeared in the doorway. "I checked the garage. The camel is gone."

George rushed outside, looking for any footprints the camel may have left behind, but there was nothing, and not knowing what else to do, he started walking around the house, searching for any clues as to what may have happened. He ventured out into the desert, but find no sign of lucy, he headed inside the house.

"I should go to the oasis," he insisted, but Jean shook her head.

"Let's give her a little while longer; perhaps she just needed some time on her own." She glanced up at her son with tears in her eyes. "I don't want to risk losing you too."

"But I could be finding her and bringing her back right now!" George yelled, the stress of the last couple of days finally getting too much for him.

Just then the sound of hooves reached them from outside, and looking out the window, George saw several riders on horseback. "Look!" he said as his family gathered around. Only

Laila and Prince Kinan – who had come downstairs once he realised Lucy was missing – stayed at the kitchen table.

"Be careful," warned Jean, "they could be robbers."

Mary sighed. "Not this again – not everyone's a criminal, you know!"

They watched as one of the riders dismounted and walked to the front door. He shouted something in Ancient Egyptian, and both Prince Kinan and Laila shot up from their seats.

"They're looking for the prince," Laila told them. "They're his guards!"

Laila ran over to the front door, and once she'd opened it, several soldiers with swords across their bodies walked into the house. When they saw the prince, they knelt down on the floor.

"I wish I got welcomed like that wherever I went," commented Mary, who was very impressed by the prince's guards.

"Kinan," George said as the soldiers stood up again, "I mean, *Prince* Kinan…" He turned to address Laila. "Could you ask him, does he think his guards could help us find Lucy?"

"Of course," Laila said, and after talking to him and turning back to George, she said, "it would be his pleasure."

And with that the prince turned to his royal guards, giving them instructions in his language as they listened intently.

So, after the horses had had a drink from a bucket of water provided by George, they split up into three groups, all heading off in different directions to try and track down Lucy.

The family waited in the kitchen with bated breath, and after an hour or so they heard the sound of horses' hooves coming up to the house again. George stood up and ran outside, and when he saw his sister on the camel riding next to the guards, he yelled at the top of his voice, "Mum! They found Lucy!"

Everyone ran outside, and once Lucy had climbed down off Cammie, Jean and Mary brought her in for a big hug.

"I'm so glad you're OK!" Jean exclaimed. "Thank God!"

After talking to his soldiers, Prince Kinan walked over to them. He spoke to Laila and she translated: "They found her wandering around in the desert. It had got so cloudy it was hard to see, and although Lucy here was frightened when she first saw the guards, she soon realised they were there to help."

Lucy smiled as she whispered a quiet, "Thank you." She was so happy to be home, although if truth be told, she also felt a little silly for getting lost in the first place. She decided she wasn't going to tell her family about the quicksand, or the hyena or the robbers, so when her mum asked her where she'd been, Lucy shrugged. "I don't know, I just got lost. I'm sorry."

Jean hugged her again as tears filled her eyes. "I'm just glad you're safely back home."

The prince said something to Laila, and she turned to the family to translate again. "The prince wants to thank you for your hospitality, but now that Lucy has been found and his soldiers are here, he must be going."

Prince Kinan waited until Laila had finished before speaking to her again, and she shrugged, as though uncertain about something. They spoke for a while, and then Laila turned to George. "I'm sorry," she said, "but my family… I'm needed."

George nodded. "I understand. I'll miss you… but I get it. I hope you find your brother and sisters." With that, he pulled Laila towards him and hugged her tightly. She wrapped her arms around him and tried not to cry.

After saying goodbye to the rest of the family, Laila mounted one of the soldier's horses, and together with the prince and his guards, they headed off into the desert.

The family watched them until they disappeared into the distance, and while Jean, Mary, and Lucy headed inside, George stood there for a little while longer, tears falling down his cheeks as he watched the dust settle.

That night, the family sat in the lounge in silence as each of them tried to come to terms with everything that had happened since they'd found themselves in Egypt. George in particular was the quietest of all, staring into space as he tried to remember every detail of Laila's face – he never wanted to forget what she looked like.

As the evening wore on the sky got darker and darker, and soon they started to hear the rumblings of thunder in the distance, followed shortly afterwards by several bolts of forked lightning that lit up the room through the drawn curtains.

Jumping up from her seat, Lucy informed everyone she was going to sleep, and after running up to her room, she took the stone tablet out from under her bed and dropped it into the bucket of water.

She'd been waiting for this weather for days, and now it was here she didn't want to risk losing the opportunity, so standing over the bucket, she quickly said, "Ahora, Ahora, Ahora!"

She thought briefly of her street back home, but then shook her head as a cheeky smile graced her lips. Actually, she thought to herself, after all this heat and sand, what she really wanted was to go somewhere cold – somewhere *really* cold.

After saying of her wish, she slipped into bed and waited for morning.

She couldn't wait to see what the next day would bring.

PART 2

Frozen land

13

EARLY IN THE MORNING LUCY WAKES UP, SHIVERING FROM cold. She gets out of bed and looks out the window. She is shocked to see that everything covered in snow. "My wish came true! There's snow everywhere!" she exclaims happily. Excited, she rummages through her wardrobe and puts on winter clothes and her big, furry boots. She rushes down the stairs and opens the front door to reveal snow, six inches deep.

"Wow," she says as she looks around. "I wonder where we are now."

The snow is so deep that she can hardly walk, but still she looks around in amazement. Lucy now notices their house is at the top of a hill that is surrounded by huge mountains. After a while of exploring and looking around, she starts to shiver from the cold and goes back inside the house. She runs upstairs to her mother's bedroom and wakes her up by shouting: "Mum! Mum! Wake up! There's snow! We're covered in snow!"

Jean, shivering in bed, gets up and says, "Oh, it's so cold. How is there snow in the desert?"

At that moment, Mary gets up as well. She grabs a blanket nearby and wraps herself in it. She goes to Jean's room and says, "It's very cold today. It must be winter season."

George, hearing the voices from Jean's room, gets up as well and also wonders why it is so cold. Lucy says, "Mum, come down the stairs and go outside. The snow is covering everything."

Jean opens her curtains and looks out. She says, "You're right. Everything is covered in snow."

None of them, apart from Lucy, know they are in another place, that they are not in the desert anymore until, that is, they go outside. Jean goes out and, like Lucy, is shocked at the sudden change in climate and location. "Where did all these mountains come from? Where are we now?" she exclaims, confused.

Mary puts on her boots and comes out to have a look as well. She is taken aback by the new environment. She takes a few steps into the snow, stumbles and falls. "How did we end up here?" she asks. Her mouth opens wide in shock. Jean rushes to her and helps her up.

"Go inside, Mum, you'll catch a cold," Jeans says to Mary.

Mary says, "It must be Christmas. That's why it's so cold."

At this point, George comes down the stairs, and jumps into the snow with a massive grin on his face. "This is so cool!" he says. He then looks around and does a double take, realising he is in a different place. "How did we end up here?" he asks Jean.

"I have no idea, George. I think we are all in a dream," she answers him.

After they all start shivering, they go inside and sit around the dining table. Jean says, "Listen everybody, this place is the complete opposite to the desert. There is enough water here, but we need to keep ourselves warm in this weather, so we need to start looking for wood and timber as soon as possible or we'll freeze to death. Luckily, we have enough food to last us a few days and we don't need a fridge because it's so cold. My mum and I will clean the fireplace and George, you and Lucy will go and collect some timber. We desperately need it."

Lucy and George nod at Jean and say, "Okay, Mum."

"Remember to wear hats, gloves, scarves to keep you warm. Go now and find all your warm clothes," Jean tells them.

George and Lucy go to their rooms and change their clothes and put on warm coats and boots. George gets his gun, and then he goes to the garage to get a wood saw, the sled, and an axe. He notices the camel is not there. Lucy goes to the gun case and takes a pistol, despite her mother telling her she shouldn't. She goes downstairs. George says to her, "The camel isn't in the garage."

"Oh, no!" Lucy says. "It's all your fault. You forgot to put it in and tie it up."

Jean, who has heard them, says, "It doesn't really matter, the camel can't survive in cold climates anyway."

George says, "Okay, Lucy, let's go."

"I'm ready," says Lucy.

"I can see the trees from here," George tells Lucy, so they trudge through the snow all the way from their house to the trees.

Whilst walking towards the trees, Lucy falls multiple times because of the thickness of the snow. "This snow annoys me so much," Lucy says. "We should wear shoes that don't sink."

George says, "Come on, stop nagging."

After a while, they reach the trees. While George cuts the dry branches with the saw and the axe, Lucy collects it all and places it on the sled. George is cutting a branch but he stops when he hears growling nearby. He looks around and sees a massive bear rushing towards him. George runs to Lucy, who is about twenty metres from him, but is unable to take his shotgun because he left it on the ground few metre away from where he was cutting the branches. As George runs towards Lucy, the bear chases him only few paces behind. "Run! Run Lucy!" George shouts, "There's a bear behind us!"

Lucy, who sees the bear behind George, hurries to get the pistol she has brought and starts shooting near the bear to scare it off. Hearing the noise, the bear scampers off in fright. George is frightened, sweating and shaking, and says, "That was so close. He almost got me."

Lucy says, "Now you owe your life to me. What would you have done if I wasn't here?"

George, slightly embarrassed, says, "I left my gun behind the tree; I didn't have the opportunity to use it. I didn't even think for a minute that there would be a wild animal in this place."

Lucy says mockingly, "Sounds to me like you're making excuses."

"Didn't Mum tell you not to take the pistol?" George asks her.

"Well, imagine if I hadn't taken the pistol with me, what would have happened to us? Please don't say anything to Mum," Lucy says.

George says, "I don't know why I look down at you; you're a very brave girl, you should be proud that you saved us."

Lucy smiles and says, "This is the first time I've received a compliment from you." She then says, "We better hurry up and get back home before Grandma and Mum freeze to death."

They both carry the sled, filled with wood, back home. When they reach the house, Lucy gets inside and says, "Mum, Mum, a wild bear attacked us today."

Jean says, "Oh, my god, what happened?"

"George shot towards the animal and it ran away," Lucy explains to her.

"Thank god, George was there to help you," Jean says.

Lucy, upset, puts her head down and says nothing. At this moment, George comes inside with the wood and takes it to the fireplace. After a while, they make the fire and put the kettle on to make tea. Jean says, "Children, I think we're going to need more wood. In this cold, we're going to use a lot of timber."

Lucy says, "Mum, right now we're tired, we'll collect wood another day."

In the afternoon, after lunch, Lucy and George take the sled to go outside, play with the snow and go sledding. They start sledding from the hill that the house is on. Lucy is sitting at the front of the sled while George pushes the sled off the hill and jumps in the back. As they are sledding down, Lucy shouts, "No one can go as fast as us!"

George is also shouting happily, "I love this place!"

As they are sliding down the hill, they hit a bump, which sends them flying into the opposite hill and about a metre deep in the snow—exactly where a polar bear is looking after its cubs. It takes Lucy and George a few minutes to get out of the snow and recover. Lucy says, "Look what you've done. You'll never be a good driver."

George hears the growling of the bear coming from inside the snow hill they had just crashed into. George shouts, "Lucy, come on! Let's get out of here! I think there's something dangerous in there."

Quickly, George digs the sled out of the hill, tells Lucy to jump in it, and then starts pushing the sled down the slope. While he does this, the angry bear tears out of its shelter and starts running towards them. Lucy, who is at the front of the sled, looks back and screams, "George, she's behind us!"

Just then, George jumps to the back of the sled and, because the slop is steep, they sweep down it and away from the bear's reach. The bear, tired of chasing them, retreats back to her cubs. When George and Lucy reach the bottom of the hill, they sigh with relief. "Thank god we made it," they say. Then they walk back home. When they get to the house, Lucy says, "Mum, we had a very exciting day. We enjoyed ourselves very much."

George nods his head in agreement and doesn't say a word about what just happened, not wanting to scare their mother.

"I'm so glad you're having a good time here," Mary says to them. "But I'm freezing. The cold is going to be the end of me."

"Don't worry, I know what you mean. We'll try our best to keep you warm and happy," Jean assures her. "The same way we managed to survive the heat. We can survive the cold as well. I keep asking myself, why did this happen to us? Why do we keep moving from place to another? I think God is testing us. We must have done something wrong to end up here." She holds Mary's hands and says. "Don't worry. Together we'll make it."

Lucy, who was listening to her mother say these words, knew that it isn't God's punishment, but the short, old man's doing. She says nothing in case she herself gets punished.

Mary says, "Okay, let's just make dinner and forget about this problem."

The next day, Lucy and George say goodbye to their mother and grandma and go out hunting again. They see a herd of reindeers and decide to approach them. George takes his shotgun from the sled and hides behind a rock. He shoots at one of them. The rest flee in fear. Lucy drags the sled to the fallen deer and together they heave it onto the sled and walk home. On their way, Lucy says, "it was a good day, but I wish Cammie was here. We could have ridden on him instead of walking."

That night, they make a great fire and have an indoor barbeque. They light dozens of candles around the house so they aren't in pitch black and then start eating. They made tea after dinner. While having their drinks, they hear the front door creaking. Jean looks at George and asks him, "Did you not close the door?"

"I thought Lucy closed it; she came in after me," George says.

Just then, a dog slowly creeps inside and pads over to the fireplace. The sudden entrance of the dog makes everybody jump with surprise and fear. George runs upstairs to get his gun. Lucy jumps on the table. Jean grabs a broom and shouts: "Get out of here!" Mary is the only person who has no reaction, as she had not seen the dog. George gets the shotgun from the case and rushes down the stairs to shoot the dog, but Jean says, "George, don't shoot. I think he's a domestic dog. He doesn't seem to be dangerous. It must be the cold weather that forced him to come here."

Lucy, who is standing on the dining table, says, "Oh, poor dog, it must be so cold and hungry." She gets down and takes a piece of meat, and lays it in near the dog. She then strokes the dog's fur. "Oh, he must be domestic, he's so nice," Lucy says. "I'm going to call him Desperate."

Mary says, "That's the perfect name for this dog. He must have been so desperate to come here, otherwise he wouldn't have."

George says, "We can take it with us when we go hunting."

"This dog has a name, George, call him by his name," Lucy says defiantly.

"Okay, fine, I'll call him Desi," says George.

Jean says, "Who would be so cruel to leave this dog outside in this weather?"

The next day, George and Lucy are playing with Desi when a beautiful bird swoops down and sits on top of a small hill that is surrounded by pine trees. George says, "Oh, I love this bird; I want to capture it and keep it as a pet at home." Then he runs home to look for a net. He finds it and says to Lucy, "Please take the dog inside the house. I don't want him to make any noise, otherwise the bird will fly off."

Lucy does what he says, taking the dog inside, but she takes her pistol with her when she goes outside to watch what George does. George quietly crawls on his hands and knees, careful to make sure the bird doesn't see him, then lowers his whole body on the ground and shuffles toward the bird. He is feeling incredibly cold as his whole body is immersed in the snow. As he is crawling, he cautiously moves aside the bushes to get to the bird. Soon he is close enough to the bird to throw the net, but the minute he lifts the net to capture the bird, he hears a shot. He looks toward the direction it came from. He sees Lucy with a pistol in her hands, laughing. Lucy calls, "I don't like birds being kept in a cage."

George is furious as he races towards her. "This time I really am going to kill you," he shouts.

Lucy then runs back into the house, screaming, "MUM! GEORGE IS GOING CRAZY! HE'S AFTER ME!" She tears up the stairs into her bedroom and locks the door.

George, while racing after Lucy, says to himself, "Why me? Why does she keep bothering me? I can't take it anymore."

When he storms into the house, he screams, "Where is she? Where is she?"

"Calm down, George. What happened with you two?" Jean asks.

Instead of answering her, George runs upstairs to Lucy's room, kicking and banging on her door, willing her to open it. He shouts, "I'll kill you this time! Why would you do that to me? It took me so long to get close to that bird! You ruined everything!"

Jean follows George up the stairs and shouts at George. "Stop that! I'm getting fed up with you two always arguing," she says. "You don't mean to kill her George, why would you say that?"

George, who had calmed down a bit, says, "I don't know why she does stuff like this to me. She doesn't respect me." He sits at the top of the stairs and with tears in his eyes says, "Mum, I'm fed up. I miss my friends in America. I want to go back home."

Jean sits beside him, hugs him and says, "I know what's bothering you. You're still thinking about Laila. I know it's not easy to completely forget her. She's got her own life so now you should think of your own future. Please don't work yourself up too much."

The next day, when everything had calmed down, George and Lucy took the sled and the dog with them to hunt. On their journey, Lucy says sorry to George for what she did. This time, they took a different route. After a while, they see a deer, munching on leaves of a bush. George slowly edged closer to the deer, making sure the snow didn't crunch too loudly under his foot. He shoots the deer and Lucy drags the sled to put the deer on it. They do this together and drag it back home. As they did this, they hear howling of a pack of wolves, which were following them. "Hurry up, we have to move fast," George says to Lucy. He tugs on the rope of the sled to get home quicker.

"You have a gun, why don't you use it to stop them following us?" Lucy asks him.

"There are so many of them. If I need to use it, I will, but right now we don't," George replies.

Desi, used to this environment, strolls calmly beside Lucy and George until two wolves get close to them. He runs toward the two wolves to stop them in their tracks and scare them away. Lucy then shouts for Desi to come back. Desi, after making sure the wolves had gone, runs back to Lucy and George. Lucy strokes the dog's head and says, "Thanks for helping us, but I don't want to put your life in danger unless it's necessary."

George then says, "It's a dog's duty to look after its owner, Lucy. We better carry on moving before the wolves come back again."

On their way back, they take a wrong turn and end up taking a different route where they see a cottage in the distance. George says, "Let's go and see who lives in that cottage. We'll probably find some good neighbours."

"I doubt it, but let's find out," says Lucy. Then they walk towards the cottage. When they get close, they notice Desi's strange behaviour. He's whimpering and retreating and now he stops in his tracks, not wanting to go any further. Lucy, not understanding what's happening to him, strokes Desi, encouraging him to carry on. They get even closer to the cottage and see a big man chopping wood with an axe. His name is Tom and he and his brother David are smugglers. It is they who live in the cottage.

George gets close to Tom and says, "Hello, do you speak English?"

Tom, who is busy cutting the timber, does noticed George, but once he lifts his head to look around, he sees George, Lucy, and the dog and says, "Who are you? What are you doing here?"

"My name is George and my sister is Lucy," says George. "We've come from America. To be honest, we don't know how we ended up here, but we live close by so we're neighbours." GEORGE and LUCY didn't know they are in 18th century CANADA.

Tom smiles and says, "So, you're my neighbours." He walks towards George and Lucy and notices the dead deer on the sled. When Desi sees Tom, he walks backwards and hides behind Lucy.

"Who hunted the deer?" Tom asks them.

"I did," George tells him. "I shot it with my gun."

Tom says, "You must be wealthy to have a gun like that. There is hardly anyone with a gun around here. We usually hunt with a bow and arrow and traps." He points to the gun on George's back and says, "I've never seen such a beautiful gun. It has been crafted amazingly. Can I try it?"

Lucy, who is hesitant to be friendly with the big man, says, "Sorry, we haven't got time. We have to go, our mum is expecting us." She tugs the back of George's jacket to get him to move. Just then, Tom sees Desi and realises he is one of his dogs. Tom looks at Lucy and says, "Where did you find this dog?"

"He is our dog, living in our house," Lucy says.

Tom laughs and says, "This dog has lived with me for a few years. I punished him because he wasn't doing his job properly. Since the punishment, two or three weeks ago, I hadn't seen him until today. Anyway, thanks for bringing him back to me."

Lucy is getting upset by what he's saying and says, "I told you, this is our dog and I don't think he enjoys being here with you. Come on, George. Let's go, Mum is waiting for us."

Just as George is about to say goodbye to Tom, the man shouts, "Who do you think you are? You come to my land. You hunt my deer. You take my dog." He storms to the sled, lifts the deer from it, and takes it with him into the cottage. George and Lucy are frozen in shock. They don't know what to do or how to respond to the situation. Tom forcefully says, "This deer belongs to me and all this land belongs to me. Anytime you want to hunt, you have to have my permission."

He then looks at Desi and shouts, "Get to the back of the house. You need a good punishment."

George says, "We thought this land wasn't owned. We didn't expect anyone to live here."

"He's obviously lying, let's go George," says Lucy. They walk off disappointed, with Desi in tow. As they turn their backs to Tom, he screams after them: "Remember that dog is mine. Next time I see you, I'll take him too!"

Still walking away from the cottage, Lucy calls out without turning back, "You must be joking."

She looks at George and says, "Don't you think we should have done something to stop him taking the deer?"

"Don't be silly, he could have been telling the truth about owning the land," George snaps.

After a while, Tom's brother David who is not in a good shape and fat arrives at the cottage with the sled, carrying building items, and some food. He says, "I brought what you asked for."

He sees the deer on the floor and says, "At last you managed to hunt a deer. We're going to have a nice dinner today."

Tom says, "We have a rich neighbour, who just moved here recently. We should go and visit them. I loved the gun that boy was carrying, and I want it."

"I hope they have other valuables as well," says David. They both laugh manically and haul the deer inside the cottage.

That day, Lucy and George come home empty-handed and, because they don't want to upset their mum, they say nothing about their bad experience with the neighbour.

Jean tells them not to worry that they hadn't hunted any-thing. "We still have enough food," she says. They all go sit at the dining table and have dinner and tea.

The next day, George and Lucy go to hunt again, but this time, they don't go near Tom's cottage. Instead, they journey towards the lake that is completely frozen. When they get to it, they make holes in the ice to catch fish with the fishing rod and hook they have brought with them. Their fishing turns out to be successful; they catch many fish. Lucy spots a few pheasants milling around the edge of the lake. She nudges George and points to them. "We better hunt some of those birds," she says.

George nods and gets his gun from the sled. He tiptoes towards the birds, careful not to make a lot of sound, positions his gun and shoots a few of them before they manage to get away. As he is shooting them down, Desi runs to collect them and bring them back to Lucy, who then ties them to the sled. While George and Lucy are hunting, Tom and David are out looking for their house. Tom notices out of a chimney and realises it is from the house they are searching for. Thrilled, they move towards it. "Look, what a nice and big house it is," Tom says to David. "I've never seen such a house before."

"They must be incredibly rich," says David. "We can probably find some expensive jewellery here." Tom reaches the front door of the house and knocks on it three times. Jean opens it up.

"Hello, we're neighbours. I'm here to welcome you," says Tom, with a fake grin on his face.

Jean says, "I'm very happy to meet you, please, come in."

Tom and David enter the house and look around in wonder. "What a beautiful house you have. There's nothing like it in this area," David says.

Mary appears and says, "I'm very glad you're here. At last we have people nearby to talk to."

Mary announces she's going to make some tea and rushes off to the kitchen. Jean tells their visitors to sit down. "How long have you been here?" she asks the brothers. "What country is this?"

Tom, who is slightly puzzled by the last question, says, "Well, it's obvious we're in Canada. We've lived here for a very long time. What about you, how long have you been living here? When and how did you build this house without us noticing?"

Jean replies, "It's a long story. We've been here for a short amount of time, but honestly, we have no idea how we ended up here."

At this moment, David gets up and starts wandering around the house. He sees the TV and asks, "What's this?"

"That's a television. It shows images of different things in a sequence," Jean says.

Tom then says, "How does it show pictures?"

"Unfortunately there's no electricity, so I can't show you," says Jean.

"Electricity? What is that?" Tom asks.

At this time, David goes up the stairs and checks all the room to see what they had. Mary then shouts, "Come on, the tea is ready!"

Suddenly, they hear something shatter, and they look up towards the noise. David has broken the gun case and has taken two of the guns. He shouts, "I found them!"

Jean furiously says, "They're not yours. Put them back!"

Then Tom takes a knife from his pocket and threatens Jean. "Do not interfere, or I'll kill you," he says.

Mary is shaking. She says, "Oh, my god, they're thieves! I wish I hadn't made tea for them."

With a rope, David and Tom tie up Jean and Mary, and then start taking anything that looks valuable and carries it all to the sled. After ransacking the house, they taunt, "We're glad to meet you," and then leave.

"I'm such a fool to have opened the door not knowing who they were. I always tell George and Lucy to check who it is before they open the door, and I made that stupid mistake myself!" Jean cries hysterically.

Trying to reassure her, Mary says, "Don't worry; I thought they were nice people, too. Don't blame yourself."

After a while, George, Lucy and Desi, arrive home with the fish and birds they caught and find, to their surprise, that their front door is wide open. George rushes inside the house to see his mum and grandma's hands and legs tied with rope. He rushes to get a knife and cuts the rope away. "What on earth happened?" he asks.

Jean says, sobbing, "I'm sorry. I shouldn't have opened the door. Two burglars came and stole everything of value as well as the two shotguns."

Lucy goes inside as well and looks around at the mess. Her mouth falls open in shock.

"They didn't harm you, did they?" George asks.

"No, don't worry, they didn't," says Jean.

Lucy says, "What are burglars doing in the middle of nowhere?" She kneels in front of her mother and hugs her tightly.

George heads up the stairs and checks the gun case. He says, "They've taken two shotguns. I hope they haven't taken the bullets." He goes to the garage and checks to see if the bullets are still there. They are. He goes back to his family and tells them the thieves haven't taken any of the bullets.

"I don't know how they'll use the guns without bullets," Lucy says.

Mary says, "I feel more sorry that they took the statue that I bought for Lucy's birthday more than anything."

"Okay, let's stop talking about what they've taken. The main thing is that we're alive and not hurt. Now we better carry on with our lives, Jean says.

"Mum, at least something good happened today. We caught some fish and a few birds," says George in an effort to lighten the mood.

Jean says, "It's so nice that we get to taste fish. We haven't had it in a while."

Mary says, "I love fish, too. Thanks kids for catching them."

Later, Jean and Mary prepare the fish and cook them. When having dinner, George and Lucy start talking about Tom. They say it must be his doing as there is no one else nearby. That night, after dinner, Lucy goes to George's room and says, "We have to do something about this."

"Yeah, I need those guns back," George replies. They start planning how they will take back what the burglars have stolen from them.

The next day, Lucy and George tell Jean they are going to collect wood. Then, together with Desi, they leave the house and head to the cottage. When they reach the cottage, they find Tom outside chopping wood. David is there, too, fixing the sled. As they get closer and closer, one of Tom's dogs starts barking loudly. Tom turns to see George and Lucy. He shouts: "What the hell are you doing here?" He hefts his axe and tears towards them, but before he can reach them, George shoots at his leg and Tom falls to the ground, crying in agony. When David hears the shot, he grabs the gun he has stolen, starts filling it with gun powder and aims at George. He pulls the trigger, but nothing happens. "These guns are useless," he shouts in fury and runs into the cottage.

Lucy strokes Desi and yells, "Get him!" Desi, glad to have this opportunity for revenge, shoots off after David. The dog jumps and grasps David's arm in his jaws. David now also screams in pain.

"You traitor!" David shouts. "Leave me alone!"

Tom gets up with great difficulty and crawls to look for his old gun, which is behind the massive pile of wood. He loads it with gunpowder and aims it at George, but George is one step ahead of Tom as he shoots at his gun, which breaks from the impact of the bullet. Tom also falls on the ground as his hand gets injured from the gun shattering.

"Save me from this dog," David yells, "I'll give back whatever I stole from you."

Lucy, hearing this from David, calls to Desi to come back. David then gets up and goes into the cottage to bring out everything he stole from Lucy's house.

"I hope you don't repeat this again," Lucy tells him. She and George pile everything on the sled and go home.

Tom, who is writhing in pain, looks furiously after them and screams, "Nobody can escape my revenge. Beware!"

George and Lucy take no notice of Tom's shouting as they go on their way back home. When they reach the house, they tell their mother and grandma that they have retrieved everything the brothers stole. Their eyes light up with joy and relief.

The next day, Lucy and George decide to go and hunt. They go towards the hills near the frozen sea, but this time they leave Desi at home to protect their mum and grandma in case the brothers came back. After some time of hiking up the hills, Lucy notices a flock of birds. She turns to George and says, "This time, I want to hunt."

George gives her his shotgun, but before he puts it in her hands, he says, "I'll give it to you, but you need to listen to me when you're shooting."

Lucy takes the gun and aims at the birds. She shoots but misses. The noise scares all the birds and they flutter away. As the birds fly off, Lucy aims at them again. She manages to shoot one, and it falls to the ground in a heap. Although her shoulder hurts from the recoil of the gun, she doesn't let it show. She looks at George and says, "See, I can hunt just as well as you can. Go and get the bird before the wolves grab it."

George, a stick in his hand, moves towards the fallen bird to pick it up. As he stoops to grab it, a polar bear appears from behind the hill. When he notices it, he runs back to her, shouting, "SHOOT! SHOOT!"

Lucy, who is now sitting on the sled, hears George's shouting. She jumps up to see the white bear following her brother. She panics and picks up the gun beside her. She shoots but nothing happens. There are no more bullets in the gun. Oh, god, she thinks. She looks around the sled for more bullets but doesn't find any. As George gets closer to her, Lucy calls out, "There aren't any bullets in the gun! I can't find any here!"

At this moment, George reaches her and says, "Never mind, just get in the sled." Lucy gets in and George pushes it from behind. Just as it begins to slide down the hill, George leaps into the back, which propels the sled forward. Lucy she realises that, in her rush, she left her gun behind on the hill. As they slide down the hill, the sled hits a bump, and they ricochet in another direction, heading taking towards the sea. About two hundred metres of the sea was completely frozen and they slide onto it until they slow to a stop. They quickly get off the sled and look back. Lucy shouts, "That bear is still following us, it must be really hungry."

George says, "Lucy, we better hurry up and jump on one of the icebergs. I don't think he'll manage to follow us onto it."

"Are you sure?" Lucy asks.

"Hurry up, we don't have time," George replies. Then they jump on the iceberg near them, taking the sled with them. The iceberg is small, no more and two-by-two. George, stick still in hand, pushes the iceberg, hoping it will move. Lucy starts paddling with the sled. At that instant, the bear gets closer to them. As they move away on the iceberg, the bear jumps into the water and follows them. When they realise the bear is still following them, they starts paddling even faster. Lucy is nagging, saying, "You idiot. You said he wasn't going to follow us in the water."

George says, "We didn't have another choice." Just then the bear gets even closer and tries to jump onto their iceberg. George starts hitting the bear with his stick, panicking. Lucy throws small pieces of ice at the bear whilst shouting: "Leave us alone! Go away!" But the bear doesn't give up. Still in the water, the bear tries to attack them again. George hits the bear on the head with all his might. The bear roars in pain and retreats. George and Lucy sigh in relief and relax on the iceberg for a few moments.

"I never heard of a polar bear not being able to swim," Lucy says, mocking George.

"Sorry, I didn't think he'd follow us into the sea," George says.

"Look, this iceberg is taking us completely away from the bank," Lucy points out.

"It's the current in the sea," George replies.

Lucy says, "I don't know which one is worse, the bear following us, or us moving far from the bank. If we don't get help, we'll freeze to death on this iceberg."

George reassures her, "Don't worry, we'll get through it."

After a few hours of wandering around the sea, George spies a rowboat near them. Both of them start shouting. The old fisherman on the boat notices them and rows toward them. "What are you doing on that iceberg?" he asks them.

Lucy says, "It's a long story. Can we get into your boat, please?"

The old man says, "Of course you can get in. You're lucky to be alive on that thing."

The old fisherman introduces himself. His name is James. George and Lucy also introduce themselves and tell him the story of the bear chasing them.

"I hardly see any strangers in this place," James says to them, "My wife and children will be happy to meet you. I had a good day today. I caught enough fish so we can have a great supper."

Then they all row towards the fisherman's home. They come out of the sea and onto the edge of the river where James' cottage is situated. After a few kilometres, they reach the cottage. There is an eight-year-old girl and a five-year-old boy on the bank of the river, waving their hands to greet their father. Lucy, George, and James all get off the boat and James ties the boat to a pole with rope. James goes over to his children and cuddles them. He gestures to George and Lucy to go inside. The little children ask their names. George points to himself and says, "My name is George." He points to Lucy and says, "This is my little sister, Lucy." Lucy smiles at the children and asks, "What are your names?"

The little boy says, "My name is Tony."

The little girl says, "My name is Margaret."

Just then, James says, "Okay, let's get inside; it's freezing out here." They all go into the cottage. The cottage is small. It has only one storey and two bedrooms. The main space is a living room, kitchen and dining room all together, with a fireplace in the far corner. On this fireplace, there is a kettle boiling. Linda, the fisherman's sixteen-year-old daughter, is preparing food and tea. She sees her father and their guests and says, "Hello" to them. James tells George and Lucy that Linda is an amazing cook. He looks at Linda and says, "We have guests. Can you make them some delicious food?"

Linda blushes with embarrassment. "Father, we don't have anything nice to give them," she says.

The fisherman laughs and says, "Don't worry. I had a great fishing day. I caught loads of fish. By the way, how's your mother feeling?"

Linda says, "She's feeling a bit better today."

James says to George and Lucy, "Okay, I'm going to see my wife. Linda will look after you."

After James goes to see his wife, Lucy and George begin to talk to his children. Lucy is talking and joking with Margaret and Tony. They ask her about her clothes and where she came from. George is talking to Linda. He asks, "It must be hard to live here, right?"

Linda says, "It is extremely hard, especially since my mother became ill. Where do you live?"

"We live a few miles away in the hills. We moved here recently," George replies.

Linda makes them some tea, pours it in wooden cups and hands it to George and Lucy while they sit at the dining table that is made out of wooden logs. Lucy says, "I've never had tea in a wooden cup before."

Linda says, "In this place we have no access to shops, or anything really. We usually make most our stuff ourselves."

She looks towards George and asks, "How did you end up here?"

George doesn't respond because he is so fixated on Linda, so Lucy looks at him and says, "Didn't you hear what she said?"

George jolts and comes to his senses. "Sorry, what did you ask?" he says.

Linda smiles and goes towards the fire to make something. Lucy says to George, "You've lost your concentration today, haven't you?" She then goes to play with the children.

At this moment, James comes out of his wife's room, takes some of the fish he caught and hands them to Linda, telling her to cook it.

The meal does not take long, and they all sit around the table, eating their supper. James says to George and Lucy, "Explain to us how you came here and where you live."

George says, "Me and my sister live in America, but somehow we came here. We don't know how. We just woke up one morning and we were on top of the hills. Our mum and grandmother are there, waiting for us right now."

Lucy, who doesn't want George to say how they ended up here, interjects. "We came here for a winter holiday and after a while we'll go back home."

James says, "I hope you enjoy your stay here. I would like to come and visit your house and meet your family."

George says, "I heard from Linda that it's very difficult to live here and find something to eat."

"Yes. A year ago, the fish were plentiful. Now I rarely catch much. It could be because of my age, but I do the best I can to look after my wife and children," replies James.

"Why don't you hunt deer and birds if catching fish is getting hard for you?" asks Lucy.

"How can I hunt? I haven't got any equipment. I've heard that there is a weapon that can shoot animals, but I don't know if it's true," James says.

George says, "Of course it's true. One day I'll get my shotgun and hunt a deer for you."

Happily, James says, "We've heard about these guns, but we can't afford one, but I would like to see how it works."

Lucy says, "George, we left the shotgun on the hill, remember?"

"It doesn't matter; there's no one there to take it. We can go back later and get it," says George. "We'd better go back home before it gets dark."

Just as they are about to say goodbye and leave, James' wife appears. She says hello to George and Lucy and sits near the table. "I'm sorry I couldn't look after you or talk to you. I wasn't feeling well," she apologises. "Next time you come, I'll look after you better."

George says, "Not to worry. You were very kind to us. Unfortunately, we can't stay any longer. My mum will be worried"

James' wife says, "I understand. All mothers feel the same way."

James says, "Let me come with you. It could be dangerous to get back."

George says, "Don't worry, we'll be fine. It shouldn't be too difficult to get back. We live near that big mountain which can be seen even from here." He points to it from the window to show the family. "You're tired. You have just come from fishing. You need to rest, so don't worry, we'll go by ourselves."

George and Lucy say goodbye to them and start walking back home. After a few metres, Lucy looks at George and says, "Well done, you're really brave for not asking them for help. Did you even think about what would happen if a polar bear crossed our path? How are we going to defend ourselves with only a stick and a sled?"

After walking for a few kilometres away from the cottage, they hear a wolf howling. After a while, more wolves howl in response, as if following George and Lucy. They get very close to their home and George says, "We don't have more than a hundred metres to get home." Just as he says this, three wolves attack them. Two of them attack George and one of them attacks Lucy. George defends himself with the stick. Lucy grabs handfuls of snow and ice and throws them at the wolf. One of the wolves grabs Lucy's leg and pulls her. Lucy screams, "George, help me!" But George can't help Lucy because he is fending two of the wolves off himself. Lucy's scream for help is heard by Desi, who has been prowling around inside the house. With all his power, Desi races towards Lucy's scream. He knows from the fear in her voice that Lucy is in danger. The wolf tears off the end of Lucy's trousers as it drags her. Lucy still kicks and throws snow at it. George, trying to fight off the wolves, has been hurt in a few places, and is starting to lose hope. Just as both Lucy and George are starting to give up, Desi appears, racing to the wolf that has Lucy in its grip. He fights it off, injuring the wolf, and then turns to the other two wolves. He fights them off as well, and the three wolves all run off, clearly injured, trailing blood. Lucy, who is crying, limps over to George. They both cry and hold each other. Lucy says, "I thought that was the end of us, and we didn't even get to say goodbye to Mum."

"I'm so sorry, Lucy, this is my entire fault. I should have listened to you and asked James to guide us," George says.

Then Lucy shouts for Desi, who is still going after the wolves, despite scaring them off. He comes back, and Lucy kneels down to pat and kiss him. "Thank you for saving us, Desi," she says as he licks her face.

"We better not say anything to Mum and Grandma about what happened. I don't want to make them upset," says George.

When they get inside the house, Mary and Jean are horrified by their appearance. "What happened? Where were you? Why are you so late? Where did you get these scratches?" Jean asks them, looking them over worriedly.

"It's not important, Mum. We were sliding down the hills and hurt ourselves," says Lucy. Jean gets the medical kit and applies TCP on their wounds and bandages them up. After this, Lucy and George sit at the dining table. Jean brings them a cup of tea. George looks at Lucy and says, "What a day we've had."

Mary says, "We were so worried about you."

"Sorry about that. The reason why we're late is because we met a fisherman and he took us to meet his family. We were there for a while. They're really nice people. I even invited them back here to meet you," George tells her.

Mary says, "Oh thank god, we won't be lonely again. I hope they're not like those robber brothers."

George says, "Of course, they're not like those criminals. They're a poor, respectful family. They really looked after us."

That night, because George and Lucy had dinner at James' cottage, they don't eat with their mum and grandma. Instead, they say goodnight to them and trudge up the stairs to their bedroom. Because they are so tired, they fall asleep straightaway.

The next day, George, after having breakfast, says to his mum, "I promised James, the old fisherman, that I'd hunt a deer for him and his family because they treated us so well."

Jeans says, "But your back isn't any better, George, you'll hurt yourself even more."

"It doesn't matter, Mum. It will get better soon," says George. He then goes to the gun case to get another gun, takes the sled, says goodbye to everybody and leaves the house. As he is leaving, Lucy says, "Don't forget to find the gun that we forgot to take."

"Don't worry, I won't forget," George says.

Jean says, "You seem really happy to be going back to that fisherman's cottage."

Lucy, who knows the real reason why George is happy to go back, whispers, "Here we go again."

Lucy turns to her mum and says, "Mum, I'm going to bed."

Jean says, "But Lucy, you just got up."

"I don't know, I just feel stressed out and I'm not feeling well," Lucy says.

Jean hugs her and says, "Okay, go and have a rest then."

After a while of walking, George gets to the fisherman's cottage. They greet each other and James ushers him inside to sit at the dining table and have a cup of tea with the family. James says, "We're so glad to see you, but what happened to your sister? Why didn't you bring her with you?"

"She wasn't feeling well today. I'll bring her next time," George tells him.

At this moment, Linda appears and asks George if he wants something to eat. He thanks her and says "Not at the moment."

The fisherman looks at George's shotgun and says, "Is this the gun you said can kill even the birds in the sky?"

George says, "Yes, this is the one. I'll show you how to use it." He calls for the children to come see it as well.

"As much as this is useful, it can be very dangerous as well, so you have to be very careful when you use it," George says.

After hearing this, James tells the children to move away, thinking the gun might misfire and hurt them. Then, George asks James, "Shall we go hunting?"

Just then, James' wife—who has been listening to their conversation from her bedroom—comes out and says "Hello" to George. "I'm sorry I couldn't accompany you. My husband is quite ill today; maybe it's better if you go hunting with Linda. She's a brave and clever girl. She'll probably learn quicker than her father."

"Can I really go hunting with him, Ma?" asks Linda.

Her mother says, "Yes, of course you can. Put your warm clothes on and don't come home empty handed."

Later, George and Linda say goodbye to them and go hunting.

George says, "We better go to the hill where me and Lucy forgot to take out shotgun first, then we can hunt."

"Yeah, okay," says Linda enthusiastically. "I've always wanted to go up those hills, but my father constantly tells me that it is too dangerous."

"Your father is right. We were attacked by wolves and bears in that area," George tells her. "But I'm fully prepared today, so we don't need to worry."

George asks Linda, "How do you spend your time here? Do you have any relatives or anyone near your cottage?"

"There's nothing around us except the frost. The only place that we go to shop once a year is a village that is a week's travel away. Because we don't have a sled, we don't bother to go more often," Linda replies.

George says, "How do you study here?"

Linda says, "Unfortunately, we can't study here. There's no one to teach us. Only sometimes, when he's not tired, does my father teach me how to read and write."

George gets upset at how unfortunate Linda's family are. He says, "If I find the time, I can help you with your education."

After a while of walking, they get to the place where Lucy dropped the gun. George picks it up. On their way back, Linda sees a herd of deer. George tells her to stay there as he creeps towards a deer and shoots it. Seeing George use the gun to shoot the deer, Linda jumps up and down in excitement and celebration. She runs towards George and says, "That machine made it so easy to shoot one of them down at this distance. My father uses a bow and arrow but he would always come back empty handed."

Together, they lift the deer's body and place it on the sled.

Linda says, "This is a miracle. We haven't had a deer in ages." She is so happy that she kisses George. George has not expected this and starts blushing. "I like you very much. From the first day I met you, I had feelings for you. We are going to be very good friends."

Linda smiles and says, "Now I know why my Mum wanted me to go hunting with you."

When they get back to the fisherman's cottage, the children rush outside to greet them. After they see the deer, they jump up and down with happiness. James himself comes out of the cottage, holds George and kisses him. "Thanks to you, we're going to have a barbeque tonight."

George leaves the deer to them and Linda and her mother start preparing dinner. While they are cooking, George takes his shotgun and demonstrates to James how to use it. Later, they have a nice dinner. After dinner, George invites the family to his house and says goodbye to them as he opens the cottage door to go home.

When George gets back, he tells his own family about what happened. He tells them, "I'd like to invite them here for dinner one day."

Jean says, "George, that's a great idea. You can ask them tomorrow to come and join us for dinner."

The next day, George gets up early and, after having breakfast, goes straight to the fisherman's cottage. He says, "My mum has invited you to come to our place for dinner tonight." In the afternoon, George, along with James' family, arrive at the house. Lucy, who was playing with Desi, sees them and runs toward the house to announce that their guests have arrived. Jean and Mary step out of the house to greet them. Jean tells everyone to get inside because it is so cold out, and so everyone trudges inside, grateful to be away from the cold weather.

James looks around at the house and says, "I've never seen such a beautiful house in my life. How long did it take to build it?"

Jean says, "We didn't build it. We bought it."

Mary, ecstatic to have company, says, "I never thought we'd have guests here. What lovely children you have." She starts talking to the children and being playful with them.

For a while, the guests wander around the house in bewilderment, as they have never seen such pictures or furniture. "What is this? What is that?" They keep asking. Lucy takes the younger children, Tony and Margaret, to one side and starts playing with them.

After looking around the house, everyone sits at the dining table and has tea and biscuits.

"I'm sorry we don't have enough biscuits to put in front of you. There are no shops around here," says Mary.

The fisherman's wife says, "It doesn't matter. We're just grateful to be here. We've lived her for over thirty years, and we've never had such lovely sweets. By the way, how do you get milk to put in the tea?"

Jean says, "This is powdered milk. We don't know how to get fresh milk."

George later asks Linda to go with him to his room so he can show her his pictures of America. They go upstairs to his room and George shows her the photographs. She has never seen something like this and is very excited and interested. George tells her, "I want to take a picture of the whole family."

They go downstairs; George gets a camera and takes a picture of everyone sitting at the dining table. He shows them, and they get so happy and surprised to see themselves on the camera screen. Jean shows the fisherman's wife the washing machine and dishwasher. She tells her, "This how we washed everything before."

James' wife's mouth hangs wide open in shock. "I can't believe this machine can wash clothes," she says.

Jean says, "I wish I had electricity to show you."

At this, George brings out his old tape recorder, finds some batteries to put them it, and plays music out loud. Everybody starts dancing and clapping to the music, and having a very good time. Later, they have a nice dinner together. That night, all of James' family sleep at Jean's house. The next day, after preparing breakfast for them, the fisherman's family thanks them for looking after them and for the great visit. They say goodbye and leave them. George escorts them out and tells them, "I will come visit you soon."

George and James' family exchange visits regularly for about three weeks. One day, when Lucy is playing with Desi outside, she notices Linda coming towards the house alone. Lucy knows she is coming to see George, and so she goes inside and, with an annoyed expression on her face, tells her mum "I'm tired. I'm going to bed."

Jean knows that whenever Lucy says this, there is something worrying her. She looks outside the window and sees Linda approaching the house. Jean says to Lucy, "Okay, go and have a rest."

George rushes down the stairs to greet Linda at the door. She steps inside. George makes a cup of tea for her and they start talking.

"Why did you come on your own? It's a very dangerous thing to do," George says.

"I wanted to say something to you in private," says Linda.

George grabs his shotgun and says, "Okay, I'll walk you home."

On their way, George asks, "What was the thing you wanted to tell me?"

Linda says, "My uncle and his son are coming to visit us."

"That's great that you'll have guests," says George.

"I don't know how to tell you, but my uncle has always wanted me to marry his son, and I think they're coming to engage me to him," Linda says.

George starts shuddering and doesn't talk for a while.

Linda notices George's reaction. "Don't worry," she says. "I like you so much, and I'm not leaving you for anyone else."

Hearing this, George becomes reassured. "I wish you came for something else," he says.

On their way, he teaches her how to shoot. At last they reach the cottage. George hugs Linda and says, "I love you, and I want to marry you. I'm going to tell my mum, and we're going to have an engagement ceremony in my house."

"You know I love you, but let's see what happens," Linda says.

They say goodbye to each other and George makes his way back to his house. When he gets home, he says to his mum, "Mum, I need to talk to you privately."

They go to his room and Jean asks, "What is it you wanted to tell me?"

George says, "I love Linda, and I want to marry her."

Jean is shocked. She says, "George, I know you love her, but you're too young. How are you going to look after her in this place?"

George says, "Mum, living here is much easier than living in America. Hunting one deer is enough to last us a week. Also she doesn't expect much. If I get married in America, I'd have to work so hard until I drop. You know I had girlfriends in America, and they never stayed with me for more than a couple of weeks."

"George, let me talk to my mum and see what she thinks," Jean says.

"You want to talk about my life and make decisions about my future with Grandma?" George asks.

Jean says, "Look, George, I'm in shock. I don't know what to say. We're in a place where the last thing we can think of is a wedding." She sees the look on George's face and says, "Don't worry, I'll think about it."

Jean then goes downstairs to talk to her mum, who was sitting in front of the fire in the sitting room. Jean says, "Mum, I want to tell you something, and I need to know what you think."

"Okay, I'm listening. What do you want to say?" Mary says.

Jean takes a deep breath and says, "George wants to get married to Linda. What's your opinion on that?"

"Well, good luck to them. I'd love to be a part of a big ceremony and see them together," says Mary.

"But Mum, you know we're not in America anymore. What if they have children and get ill? Who's going to help them?" Jean says.

Mary says, "Are you saying we're not going back to America? We will one day."

"I don't know, but when I asked the fisherman about America, he said the English soldiers are in charge of America and Canada. This means we are in the time where America hasn't gotten their independence yet."

Then Mary says, "I don't know about that, but one day we'll go back."

"Oh, god, I can't ask you anything, I have to make the decision myself," says Jean.

A few days pass and Lucy again, is outside the house playing with Desi, when she sees Linda coming towards the house alone. She runs inside the house and into the kitchen where she sees George. She tells him, "Your Juliet is coming."

George rushes outside and greets Linda. He says, "I told you it's dangerous to come here on your own."

He suddenly notices the tears in Linda's eyes. He hugs her and asks, "What happened? Why are you crying?"

"My father passed away." She starts crying even harder.

"I can't believe it. I'm so sorry," George says, hugging her. He takes her hand and leads her inside the house.

When they get inside the house, Jean asks George "Why is she crying?"

George says, "Her father, James, passed away."

Jean cuddles Linda and says, "I'm very sorry."

George makes some tea and brings some biscuits and sweets and puts them in front of Linda. Lucy sits on the stairs and says nothing. Mary sits beside Linda, comforting her. "I was really enjoying your father's company. Now who will look after the children?"

Jean then says, "We all better go to the cottage for the funeral."

They all prepare themselves to make their way to the fisherman's cottage. When they get there, the children, Tony and Margaret, come to greet them. They all hug and kiss them and tell them they're sorry. They do the same with the fisherman's wife. Once they get inside, the fisherman's wife says, "Luckily James' brother and nephew are here to help us. Outside we have dug the grave."

They bury the casket containing James' body. George helps Linda's uncle and cousin to lower it into the ground. The uncle then says a few words to commemorate James. After the burial, they all go inside the cottage and Jean says, "Unfortunately, we have to go back home because we can't leave the house empty. We don't want to get burgled again."

The fisherman's wife thanks them for coming and helping. She hopes they visit again. Lucy, with tears in her eyes, kisses the children goodbye. George wanted to kiss Linda goodbye, but doesn't want to do it in front of her uncle. He says, "Goodbye, I hope I see you soon."

On their way home, Lucy asks her Mum "Now who will feed the children?"

"God help them," Jean says, "They're going to have a difficult life."

The next day, Linda tells her mum, "I'm going to see George. I'll be back soon."

Her mum says, "Linda, from now on, you should stay at home and look after your uncle and cousin. It's not right that your cousin, Terry, should do everything."

Linda whines, "But I'll come back early."

"Do the cooking before you leave," her mother says.

Linda agrees and starts cooking so that she can leave as soon as possible.

She is nearly done cooking when her mum comes up to her and says, "I want to talk to you."

They go to her mother's bedroom and Linda asks, "What is it, Mum?"

Linda's mum says, "You should marry your cousin."

Linda says "Never! I love George and I want to marry him, not Terry!"

"Listen, from what I've heard, they all belong to a different world; to a world where machines wash their clothes, not human hands, and where electricity lights their house. We don't understand their world. They could go back to their own country any time. I hear them saying they wish they could go back home," says her mum.

"In that case, I wish to go with them as well," says Linda.

Linda's mum starts crying. She says, "What about us? Who will look after me and your siblings? You know I don't feel well. If you leave, we'll die of hunger. Is that what you want? You are the only one who can help us survive if you marry your cousin. If you marry him, you can stay in the cottage and look after us. He's a simple man and an experienced fisherman. He can help us a lot."

While Linda was listening to her mum, tears had filled in her eyes. No she says, "I love George and I promised I would be with him."

Linda's mum says, "I know you do. And your father was very happy about your friendship with George, but nobody thought that your father would die. Your poor father. The last thing he said before his death was 'who will look after Tony and Margaret if I die?'" She starts crying again.

Linda, with tears in her eyes, says, "Okay, Mum, don't cry anymore. I understand what you're saying. I apologise for only thinking about myself. Tomorrow I'm going to see George and tell him everything. To make sure I get home safely, I'll bring Terry with me."

The next day, Linda and her cousin make their way to George's house. When they approach the house, Linda tells Terry to wait outside and that she'll be back soon. Lucy and

George are playing with Desi outside of the house when George notices Linda coming towards them.

"Oh, my god, she's on her own again," says George and he runs to her. Lucy, who has been enjoying playing with George, knows she isn't going to see him for a while. She frowns, grumpy and upset and stomps inside the house, slamming the front door closed.

Jean asks, "Are you okay, Lucy?"

"Mum, I'm tired, I'm going to bed," is Lucy's reply.

Meanwhile, outside, George hugs Linda and says, "Why did you come on your own again?"

"There's an important thing that I want to talk about with you," Linda says.

George asks with hesitation: "What do you want to ask? You must be cold. Let's go have a cup of tea and we can talk later."

Linda says, "Sorry, I can't. I'll explain why later."

George takes his gun and follows her.

On their way, George asks: "What's happened?"

She sighs. With tears in her eyes, she says, "I have bad news. I'm sorry George, I can't marry you. I love another person."

Hearing this, George's entire body starts shaking. He sighs loudly and, with a shaky voice, asks, "What do you mean?"

"I love my cousin, and I want to marry him instead," she says.

"Why? Why would you do this to me?" George asks. "I told you that I love you and that I can't live without you. What mistakes have I done that made you change your mind?"

Linda has tears in her eyes when she says, "You haven't made any mistakes. You have been the dearest and best friend I have ever had. You taught me the enjoyment and beauty of life. Meeting you, made me hopeful about carrying on with my life but, unfortunately, I have a bigger problem."

George says, "What problem? Please tell me and I'll help you. Just don't leave me alone."

Linda moves closer to George and kisses him on the cheek. She says, "I respect you. You have a good heart, and I know you would do anything for me, but my problem is a family one. My family need me. From now on, I have the responsibility to look after my mother and siblings. You always tell me that eventually you will go back home? What will happen to me if you go?"

George replies, "Well, you can come as well."

"Then what happens to my mum and little brother and sister? They will die of hunger and cold," Linda says.

George looks away and says nothing. Tears spill from his eyes. He knows she is right, and that he cannot change her mind, and that it is not right to change her mind.

George asks, "Will I see you again?"

"My cousin is waiting for me behind this hill. I cannot leave him waiting in this freezing weather," she says. "Thanks for everything you've done for me and my family. Goodbye, my dear friend. I hope to see you again one day." With that, she walks towards her cousin.

George, tears in his eyes, is distraught. His gaze follows her as she walks to where her cousin is waiting. After a while, George remembers something and runs towards Linda. When he gets to her, she is already with her cousin. He shouts, "Wait! I forgot to give you something. I promised your father to give him a gun. Now that he's dead, I'll give it to you as a wedding present."

Linda thanks him and George says, "I wish you all the best." He says goodbye to them and turns to go home. After a while, on his way home, he reaches a small hill and looks back to see Linda and her cousin walking hand in hand. They disappear into the distance. Tears stream down George's face as he walks back home. Jean watches from the window and sees George by himself with his head hanging. She opens the door for him and asks, "Where's Linda? Why is she not with you?"

"She's not coming back Mum," George says.

"What do you mean?" says Jean.

George says, "Mum, she left me. I don't blame her, she had to."

Jean hugs him tightly and says, "I'm sorry, George."

Lucy, who was in her bedroom, listening, rushes down the stairs and hugs both her brother and mum and says, "Don't worry, George, we love you."

George says, "I think this is my destiny. I'm going to go to bed. I'm tired."

He goes to his bedroom. Jean says, "Poor George. This is not his first time having an unlucky relationship with someone. I hope he manages to sleep tonight."

The next day, George and Lucy, with Desi, go to collect wood. They are cutting branches off trees and colleting them when Tom and David come upon them. Tom says to his brother, "We should give them a lesson which they'll never forget."

David says, "But they have those miracle shotguns."

"We should kidnap that girl at the first opportunity and then, as ransom, we could ask for the guns and all the jewellery her family has," says Tom.

"Okay, that's a good plan, but how are we going to do it?" asks David.

Tom says, "You make the sled ready. We'll kidnap the girl together at the right time. Take her with you on the sled, and I'll strike a deal with her brother to free her."

Lucy and George, when they started collecting the wood, hadn't been talking to each other very much. Lucy had been checking up on him only once he'd cut the wood and she had to collect the branches. Now, George furiously hacks at the branches and throws them aside for Lucy to carry back to the sled. Lucy comes close to George and says, "I'm sorry for your break up with Linda."

George shouts at her, "Shut up and leave me alone. I don't want to hear a word from you."

Lucy, upset, moves further away from him to look for wood. The long distance between Lucy to George gives Tom and David the perfect opportunity to kidnap her. They creep slowly down the hill behind Lucy. Tom grabs her and clamps a hand on her mouth to stop her from screaming. They take her to their sled and tie her up by her hands and feet. At this moment, Desi, who is wandering around, goes to where Lucy was collecting wood and follows her scent to see where she is. He smells the scent of his previous owners and starts running to find Lucy. At this exact moment, David says goodbye to Tom. Desi reaches them and attacks Tom. Tom defends himself with a stick of wood, swatting Desi away. David takes this opportunity to run off with the sled. Desi, who knows Lucy must be in the sled, releases Tom and follows David instead.

George's head is so filled with thoughts of Linda that he doesn't hear what is going on. After filling the sled with wood for a while, he calls Lucy and Desi. He hears nothing, and so he follows Lucy's footprints. Then he notices two more sets of footprints. He panics. He guesses whose footprints they must be and becomes furious. He seizes his gun and storms towards Tom's house. When he arrives there, he pounds on the door. Tom opens the door with a smile on his face and steps out of the house. "What can I do for you, my dear neighbour?" Tom asks.

"Is my sister here?" George demands.

Tom says, "No, she's not here, but if you love her, you should do what I tell you."

George says, "What do you want?"

"I want all the things you have stolen from me, plus bullets for those guns. You didn't tell me those guns needed bullets," Tom says.

George says, "We haven't stolen anything from you."

"Those guns of yours do miracles. If I had a few of them, no one could match me here. If you miss your sister, give me whatever I ask of you, or you won't find her alive," says Tom.

George thinks for a while and asks, "How do I know you won't hurt her?"

Tom says, "Look who's talking about hurting. Have you seen my hands and legs? Can you see what you've done to me? I told you I was going to have my revenge."

George loses control, aims the gun towards Tom and says, "Tell me where my sister is or I'll kill you."

"If you kill me, you'll never find your sister," says Tom. "She is miles away from here with my brother; therefore, you better give me what I ask if you want your sister back."

When he hears this, George lowers his gun and says, "I'll talk to you about this matter later, but if anything happens to her, I'll kill you and your brother." He goes back home.

Meanwhile, Lucy is in the sled that is being pulled by a few dogs. David covers Lucy with a blanket and then guides the dogs with a whip. Lucy shouts at him, "Where are you taking me?"

"I'm taking you to a place where no one will ever find you," David says. "For your freedom, your brother needs to give us all your guns and jewellery."

Lucy says, "I'm not sure I'm not worth that much to my brother. I don't think he'll give you all those things."

"In that case, you better say goodbye to your life," says David.

Lucy is frightened, so says nothing.

George rushes home and says, "Mum, I have bad news."

Jean says, "What's happened?"

"They've kidnapped Lucy," George says with his head hung low.

"What? How! Who took her?" Jean practically screams.

George says, "Those two brothers who burgled the house. They've kidnapped Lucy. They said they want jewellery and guns as ransom. If we give it to them, we'll get Lucy back."

Mary says, "Oh, my god! Those two brothers are so dangerous. We better make a deal with them."

Jean says, "This problem doesn't need thinking. I'm ready to give everything so they can give Lucy back."

"Mum, think about it. How are we going to live without the guns? How will we defend ourselves? How will we hunt if we give the guns to those criminals? We'll die of hunger." George says.

Jean, with tears in her eyes, says, "Poor Lucy, I don't know how she's going to spend the day with them. We'll give them anything they ask, and I don't want you to discuss this matter any further."

David is driving the sled as fast as he can, but then he hits a stone and the sled flips over. Lucy falls on one side and David on the other side. The dogs stop running. David, frustrated, staggers up and checks the sled for damages A rail is broken and he starts repairing it. Lucy has also fallen onto the snow, but she can't move because her hands and feet are tied. She shouts, "Get me up! I'm going to freeze here."

David shouts back, "I'm the boss here. If I want, I'll come and help you. Now, please shut up and let me do my job."

Lucy, who is shivering from the cold, remembers she has a knife in her pocket. With difficulty, she manages to get the knife and use it to cut through the ropes around her hands and feet. She suddenly sees a dog rushing towards her. As it comes closer, she sees that it is Desi. Relieved, she hugs and kisses Desi. She says, "Desi, this isn't the time for cuddling. We need to get out of here."

Then they start running away from David, who is focused on the sled. After a while, David notices Lucy's absence and rushes to the front to untie two of the dogs. He points in the direction that Lucy is running and yells to the dogs, "Go get her!"

The two dogs begin chasing Lucy. Just then, the forest resounds with the loud howling of wolves. David is a heavy-set man and is soon huffing and puffing. Instead of going after Lucy himself, he orders the dogs to chase her. But the two dogs have heard the howling of the wolves, and are frightened. They slink back to David, tails between their legs.

Lucy's leg is bleeding from the accident with the sled. Blood drops on the ground and this prompts the wolves to follow Lucy at a distance. After a few hours of walking, Lucy becomes exhausted, so she and Desi stop for a bit. They notice smoke coming from the chimney of a cottage a few miles off behind the hill. Lucy happily looks toward the smoke, relieved that she will not die of the cold. She rubs Desi's head and says, "We should go there."

As they walk towards the cottage, one of the wolves prowls towards Lucy, but before they get to her, Desi jumps in front of Lucy and growls at the two wolves. They all pounce on each other and start fighting. The other wolf, now that Desi is distracted, attacks Lucy on its own. Lucy grabs a few stones and throws them at the wolf, all the while calling to Desi to save her. As Lucy defends herself from the wolf, it bites her hand. Lucy pulls back in agony. She screams out loud. Desi, who has fought off the wolf, runs to the wolf attacking Lucy and a fight ensues between the two. Lucy shouts and encourages Desi to beat the wolf. The wolf cannot match the strength of Desi and so retreats with the other wolves back into the trees. Lucy, who is shocked and frightened, hugs Desi tightly, thanking him for saving her. In reply, Desi licks her face enthusiastically.

"Thank god you followed me .Otherwise I would have been in the wolf's stomach," says Lucy. They start walking towards the cottage again. By the time they reach the cottage, which is at the bottom of the hill, the sun is already setting. Lucy stands before the door and looks for a bell or knocker. She doesn't find either, so she gets a stone and bangs on the door with that. A few seconds later, a fat middle-aged woman opens the door. She sees Lucy and is very surprised to see that she is alone. She peers out of the cottage to make sure Lucy is there by herself. She asks, "Have you come on your own?"

Lucy replies, "No, I've come with my dog, Desi."

The woman, whose name is Jackie, says with a mischievous smile, "What are you doing here? How did you find this place?"

"It's a long story," says Lucy. "Can we come inside? It's freezing."

"You can come inside, but I'm not going to let that dog inside my home," says the Jackie.

Lucy begs, "Please let him inside as well. It's cold outside and he must be hungry."

Jackie says, "Either you come in by yourself, or you can go back to where you came from."

Lucy, who has no other choice, reluctantly accepts. She says bye to Desi and tells him to stick around and that she won't take long. She goes inside the cottage and sits near the fireplace.

Jackie says, "You have very expensive winter clothing. You must be from a wealthy family."

Lucy, whose hands and legs are injured, asks for some bandages to cover the wounds.

Jackie sits on a chair, grabs a dirty cloth, and says, "You can use this." She throws it at Lucy. Lucy looks at the cloth and says, "I'm better off without this."

Lucy notices a pan at the fire. She says, "That smells nice. What are you making for dinner?"

Jackie says, "Dinner? This dinner is not for you. If you want dinner, you have to work for it. I don't give free dinner to anybody."

"I'm only your guest for tonight. I'll be leaving tomorrow," says Lucy.

"Why aren't you listening? If you want dinner, you have to work for it," Jackie says.

Lucy says, "But I'm tired. And my hands and legs are injured."

"I don't care about your little problems. If you want food, you have to work for it," says Jackie.

"Okay, fine. What do I have to do?" Lucy asks.

Jackie says, "You need to clean the whole house, sweep the floor, then mop it and wash all the dirty dishes."

Lucy looks around at the cottage. The place is a mess. Dirty dishes are piled high. The floor is thick with grime. She says, "It will take weeks to clean this place."

"It's up to you if you want to accept the deal or not," Jackie tells Lucy.

Lucy says, "Could I please wash the dishes first and leave the cleaning for tomorrow. I'm just so tired."

Jackie says, "Okay, I accept that, but remember you cannot leave the cottage tomorrow until it's nice and clean."

"Collect all the dirty dishes and put them on a tray. Where can I wash them?" Lucy inquires.

Jackie replies, "Not inside the house. You go outside. There's a river. You can wash them there."

Lucy takes all the dirty dishes and goes outside with them. She sits on the bank of the river and shivers. She says, "Oh god, it's freezing here." She rubs her hands together and blows on them to warm them up. She breaks the ice on the river with a stone and begins to wash the dishes. The water is so cold that every time she washes one plate, she has to warm up her hands again in order to continue. At this moment, Desi who is walking around sees Lucy and accompanies her. Lucy hugs him and says, "Lucky you don't have to wash the dishes or clothes. You only have one piece of clothing that you don't have to take off to wash or ever buy another."

After washing all the dishes, she puts them on the tray and carries them inside the cottage. She lets Jackie know that she is finished washing the dishes. Jackie then puts all the washed dishes on one side of the dining table and gives Lucy another tray of unwashed dishes. "Wash these as well," she demands.

Lucy knows she can't say no to her. With shivering hands and tears in her eyes, she takes the tray and walks back out to the river. While going back to the river, she mutters under her breath, "It's not fair," she repeats, "It's not fair."

She puts the tray beside the river. Desi comes towards her. She hugs him again, warming up her hands on his fur. Then she washes all the dishes and at last goes inside the cottage once again. She puts the clean dishes on the dining table. Then, Jackie scoops a few spoonfuls of rabbit soup into a bowl and hands it to Lucy. Lucy is so hungry that she gulps down the soup and then asks, "Please, can I have some more?"

Jackie, frowns with anger, says, "You want more?" Lucy is frightened and says nothing.

Jackie asks, "Where did you say you come from?"

Lucy says, "We have come from America. We live a few miles away from your cottage."

"This is impossible. I know everybody who lives around here, and I've never heard of you and your family. You must be mistaken," Jackie says.

Just then, Jackie goes outside to use the toilet and Lucy takes this opportunity to put some more soup in her bowl. She eats a bit, and then hides the rest in one of the rooms in the cottage. When Jackie comes back, Lucy tells her that she's very tired and that she wants to go to sleep. Jackie tells her, "Go to that small room and sleep there. Do not touch anything."

Lucy goes to the small room, which is the room where she has stashed the soup. She eats a bit more, and keeps the rest for Desi. This room, too, is a complete mess. The bed is broken and has only a few thin blankets on it. Lucy lies down for a couple of hours then, making sure Jackie is asleep, she opens the window and calls Desi, who has been waiting outside. Hearing her voice, he rushes over and jumps through the window and into the room. Lucy hugs her dog and puts the bowl of soup in front of him. Lucy tells Desi to sleep under the bed in case Jackie comes in to check on her. It is a freezing night and, as Lucy shivers while she sleeps, she thinks what a big mistake it was to wish to come to a cold place.

"Now I have to shiver 'till the morning," she murmurs to herself. She is still thinking about a plan for tomorrow when she hears thunder and sees the lightening through the window. She leaps out of the bed and looks out of the window and up to the sky. She whispers to herself sarcastically, "Thank you, what a time to have this lightening. I think everyone is against me today." With her finger pointed at the sky, she says, "I'm very cross with you." She goes to bed and says, "I hope everything gets better tomorrow." And she goes to sleep.

The next day, early in the morning, Jackie kicks the bedroom door open and wakes Lucy up. Desi is sleeping under the bed, just as Lucy told him to, and so Jackie doesn't notice him. She screams "Wake up, Princess. It's time to clean the cottage."

Lucy jumps in bed, still half asleep and says, "Okay, I'll get up in a minute."

She gets up. It takes her a minute to figure out where she is. She has slept with all her clothes on because it was so cold. She hugs Desi and tells him to stay quiet until she comes back. She goes to the dining room and sees Jackie standing up, clearly in a bad mood, staring at her. Lucy is so frightened that she doesn't look around, and so is unaware that someone is sitting in the corner of the cottage. Jackie then asks Lucy, "Do you know this man?"

Lucy looks to where Jackie is gesturing and sees David. She freezes. She can't say anything. She thinks, 'I'm finished.'

David then says, "Hello, Princess, how are you? I hope you had a nice time here."

He laughs and says, "Do you know where you are? You're in my sister's home. I knew you wouldn't get very far. That's why I wasn't rushing to find you."

He looks at his sister and tells her "I have to take her to Tom so we can act out our deal with the girl's family. You will get your share of the reward, don't worry."

Jackie then says, "Let her clean my cottage first, and then you can take her any damn place you like."

After hearing this, Lucy rushes to her bedroom and shuts the door behind her. She calls Desi and says, "It's time to go." She opens the window. At the exact moment she tries to jump out of the window, Jackie opens the door and grabs Lucy's hands and yanks her back. "Where do you think you're going? The cottage isn't clean yet," she says.

"Leave me alone!" shouts Lucy. Desi, who Jackie has not realized is there, attacks Jackie. She lets go of Lucy in fright and rushes to David for help. Lucy takes advantage of this moment and jumps out of the window, calling Desi to join her. She shouts, "Hurry up!"

As she runs, she realizes she doesn't know what direction to take as she has no idea know where she is, but the minute she sees David's sled with the dogs, she makes the decision to jump in. Lucy grabs the whip and waves it and shouts for the dogs to go, but they don't move. She begs and shouts for the dogs to move, but there is no response. Desi, guessing what Lucy wants, goes to the dogs and barks at them. Suddenly, the sled starts moving. Desi is in front of the all the dogs, guiding them. Just then, David tears out and shouts at his dogs to stop and come back. He runs a few metres after the sled but gets tired and short of breath, so goes back to his sister and tells her, "She got away. I don't know how. Those dogs don't listen to anyone except me."

"Your dogs are just as stupid as you are," Jackie says. "Now what are you going to do?"

David says, "Don't worry. I spent last night in your son's cottage fixing my sled. He said he'll come here this morning, so I can borrow his sled and get to that girl."

Suddenly, they hear dogs barking and a sled approaching. David looks at Jackie and says, "I told you he was going to come."

A few minutes later, Jackie's son stops in front of David and asks, "What's happening? Why are you outside?"

David says, "Get off. I have something really important I have to do."

He then leaps onto the sled and follows Lucy, whipping the dogs so they'll go faster. Because David is an expert at using a sled and knows the path, he catches up to Lucy in no time at all.

Lucy notices David on her tail. He is getting closer and closer. She starts shouting at the dogs to go faster. But David's skill with the driving a sled allows him to move up parallel with Lucy. He shouts, "You can't get away from me!"

He starts lashing Lucy with the whip. Lucy feeling the whip against her skin and screams in pain and then yells, "Ow! Stop it!"

David laughs and says, "Stop your sled or you'll be punished even more."

Just then, both of the sleds reach the highest part of the hill, which is so narrow it only has enough room for one sled. David, who knows the area, tries to push Lucy away. Desi tries to push the dogs from the other slide aside. He gets furious from seeing the dogs from the other sled pushing them. He starts fighting the dogs that are trying to push the whole sled away. David is on the edge of the hill. As Desi continues to fight the dogs, David's sled slips further and further towards the edge until the dogs fighting causes his sled to capsize right over. David rolls down the hill as the sled falls. He howls, badly injured. His dogs, however, stop at a short distance. Lucy sees what has happened and shrieks in joy, jumping and punching the air with her fists. "Shame on you!" she shouts, "You deserve it, you monster!"

She then directs the sled towards her house. However, because the path leads past Tom's house first, she expects more challenges. To her surprise, when she gets close to Tom's cottage, she sees George and her mum carrying the sled loaded with valuables, standing outside Tom's cottage, talking. Tom, when he sees the sled, thinks it's his brother, David, bringing Lucy and then says to Jean, "Okay, now give me everything we agreed on." He gestures to the sled. "And we'll give you back your daughter."

At that moment, Lucy shouts to the dogs to stop. They halt right in front of the cottage.

"Okay, hand me the valuables," Tom says. Suddenly, Lucy jumps off the sled and says to George, "Don't give him anything. I ran away from David."

Jean is thrilled to see Lucy and hugs her tightly. George, who was about to hand his gun to Tom, instead points it at him and tells him not to move. Lucy then says, "We better put all of this onto the sled and go back home."

As they are putting all their stuff back onto their sled and moving towards their home, Tom, who was shocked at what happened, shouts at them, saying, "These are my dogs! Where are you taking them?"

Lucy says, "Don't worry. I'll release your dogs when we get home."

Tom threatens them. "You're going to pay for this. I'm going to destroy you all," he says.

At this very moment, the sky lights up with lightening. Lucy looks up and says, "I don't think so."

Then they all move towards the house. When they get home, they have a party and start making a nice dinner. Lucy tells everyone the story of what had happened to her. Mary kisses Lucy and says, "You're a very brave girl."

Jean, who is so happy to see her daughter again, says, "I'm very proud of you, Lucy."

George apologises for not talking to Lucy before she was kidnapped.

Later, after dinner, they are so tired that they all go and have an early sleep. Once Lucy is in her bedroom, the lightning flashes again. She finds the tablet, puts it in a bucket of water and says three times, AHORA ,thinks for a second and says "Oh, god. I'm not sure now. Should I go home or not?" but immediately she makes her mind up.

She smiles and says, "I would like to go somewhere that is not too hot and not too cold. Maybe somewhere on an island with a nice climate."

Then she lies down on her bed and goes to sleep.